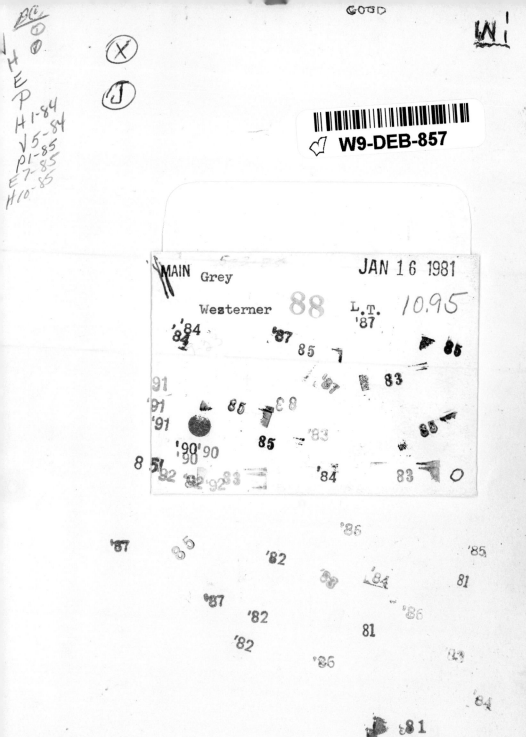

THE
WESTERNER

Also Available in Large Print
by Zane Grey:

Forlorn River
Valley of Wild Horses
The Rustlers of Pecos County

THE WESTERNER

Zane Grey

edited by Dr. Loren Grey

G.K.HALL&CO.

Boston, Massachusetts

1980

Library of Congress Cataloging in Publication Data

Grey, Zane, 1872-1939.
  The westerner.

  Large print ed.
  1. Large type books. I. Grey, Loren.
II. Title.
PS3513.R6545W4 1980   813'.52   80-24097
ISBN 0-8161-3125-2

Copyright © 1977 by Loren Grey and
Betty Zane Grosso

Published in Large Print by arrangement with
B. P. Singer Features, Inc.

Set in Compugraphic 18 pt English Times by
Debra M. Nelson

THE
WESTERNER

EXCELLENT

Chapter 1

All the way west to Reno Katherine
Hempstead had a growing realization that
her desire to save her mother from disgrace
might develop a far-reaching good for
herself.

The journey had been a revelation. She
belonged to the eastern class who preferred
to travel abroad rather than discover their
own country. The great plains, the grand
Rockies, the glorious desert had charmed
and fascinated Katherine, and finally had
awakened in her a strange longing. Had
she really ever known what it meant to be
free, alone, self-sufficient? Her mother's
ridiculous affair with the fortune-hunting
Leroyd had shocked Katherine out of her

gay devotion to amusement, and had driven her post-haste across the continent to try to prevent the impending Hempstead divorce and scandal. Long gazing from a Pullman window through saddened and thoughtful eyes had worked upon her the alchemy of wonder and discontent.

To Katherine's surprise, Reno did not disgust her. A vague anticipation of crude people, raw life, hideous buildings did not materialize. She registered at the famous Hotel Reno, where her mother and Leroyd were staying, and sallied forth to see the town, conscious of an unfamiliar sensation of excitement. It was her first experience on foot, at night, in a strange city. Unconsciously she shrank from the meeting with her mother. She wanted to compose herself to new surroundings, to a perplexing situation, to think. And to her amazement she found that the process of constructive thinking was difficult and illusive. Now there was a new sensation, not experienced since her sixteenth year. Katherine had to laugh at this, and label it as a girlish dream of adventure that never would materialize. At twenty she seemed sophisticated, worldly, old in the modern outlook on things.

It was a Saturday night in early May. She needed the coat she had put on. The air was keen, cold, sweet, but did not appear to have enough oxygen in it for her. A few blocks of quick walking took her breath. This distance brought her apparently into the center of Reno. The street was crowded with cars and pedestrians, moving under the garish red and purple Neon lights. Jazz music pealed out from somewhere. The atmosphere and brilliance were suggestive of holiday. Katherine felt it incongruous to be reminded of the Riviera, Monte Carlo, even Coney Island. Presently she grasped that the significance of this must be what she had sensed coming west, the loosening of restraint, the effect of open spaces, the spirit of play. She did not need to be told that prohibition was on its last legs.

Between almost every store and restaurant there was a garish or elaborate edifice devoted to games of chance. The names intrigued her. Golden Fleece, The Elite, Nevada Club, Last Chance, The

Show Down, were among the names she passed within two blocks. The clink of silver and rattle of roulette wheels were not unenticing to Katherine. She loved to gamble. It was in her blood. But her bridge and golf gambling, like that on board continental liners and in the gilded palaces of Europe, had been indulged in with her own class. Here if she wanted to play, it would be among a motley crowd. Her training forbade that. But as the subtle thing stirred within she yielded so far as to decide that if she could find a suitable companion she certainly would not leave Reno without taking a fling at the gambling tables.

Katherine was aware that men stared at her. Not that this was an unusual state of affairs, except that she was in a town of unknown possibilities and alone. The fact, however, that she was not accosted reassured her. Reno, she had heard, was a city where all women and especially women unaccompanied could feel safe from annoyance, and so far there seemed justification for the statement. That fact alone would be something of a novelty to

Katherine. She had never been able to escape from one of the tributes to striking beauty.

Crossing the street she suddenly surrendered to temptation, and entered the most pretentious of the gambling halls. A blaze of light and wave of sound assailed her. The place appeared to be an enormous hall, crowded by rings of men and women around the different games. She stood a while watching.

Many of the numerous people around her appeared to be merely spectators, some of them quite apparently tourists. She went closer, presently, to get a view of the players around one of the roulette wheels, and discovered men and women in evening dress at elbows with pale-faced gamblers and rough-visaged miners and ranchers.

No one appeared to notice Katherine, an omission that grew upon her and at first piqued her. So accustomed had she always been to the immediate attention that her beauty attracted, that the lack of it seemed almost strange. But when she analyzed it, it was with a growing appreciation of the new sense of freedom her apparent insignificance engendered.

Presently, when Katherine had satisfied her curiosity, she left the hall. Upon emerging on the street, she found she had become turned around and was unsure of her direction. She did not want to inquire of any of the doubtful-looking loungers lined up outside, so started walking slowly along. About half a block farther on she hailed a tall young man who looked reassuring.

"Will you please direct me to the Hotel Reno?"

"Yes, ma'am," he replied, halting. "Six squares this way."

"Thank you. I was completely turned round."

"But see heah, Lady. You cain't find it without turning off. Street's closed. There's a fire."

The shrieking siren of a fire-engine and a congestion down the street verified his statement.

"Oh! — Can I go in a taxi?" inquired Katherine.

"Sure, if you can find one."

"I'm a stranger in Reno."

"So am I. Got in today. I'm not crazy about it. My mother is at the Reno. I am going there. If you like, you can come with me."

Katherine gave him an appraising glance. He was tall and had wide shoulders. His face, cleancut and tanned, proclaimed him to be around twenty-five or twenty-six years old. She could not determine the color of his eyes, but they were piercing and troubled. They certainly were not taking stock of her. And that gave Katherine a chance for a keener glance. During the last half of her journey to Reno, she had seen cowboys, cattlemen, rangers; and this superb young Westerner belonged to this class.

"Thanks. I can risk it if you can," she replied, with her low laugh. And then she was walking beside him. Naturally she expected him to speak. But he was silent. She had to quicken her stride a little. She felt something shy or aloof about him, and she was prompted to feel him out. "Is it safe — and proper for a girl to be out alone at night in Reno?" she asked, to get his reaction.

"Safe heah, if anywhere in the West. But I reckon hardly proper."

"Oh! . . . . You see I just arrived. I wanted to look around. I walked down the street. Then I went in one of the gambling places."

Her confidences did not seem to arouse his interest or curiosity. For all she could tell, this Westerner might think she was a moving-picture actress or a schoolteacher or an adventuress, or he might not have thought about it at all. This was a new type of individual to Katherine Hempstead. She kept pace with his long stride, which she saw he at least tried to accommodate to her shorter one. And they walked on half a block in silence. Katherine could not recall when she had wanted to giggle as she wanted to now. She looked up at him and decided that she could no longer deny he was more than handsome. His hair appeared to be tawny or chestnut, and it had the little curl or wave women admired. She was struck again by an impression of trouble that emanated from him.

"Didn't you say you just arrived in Reno?" she asked, becoming uncomfortable at his protracted silence.

"Yes. This afternoon. My train was late."

"I'm from New York. Where did you come from? I can tell you're Western."

"California. But I'm not native. I was born in Arizona and lived there on a ranch till I was twenty. Then Dad sold his cattle and we went to California."

"Do you like California as well?"

"It's shore fine. But not Arizona. I caint explain."

"You miss the range?" she queried, sympathetically.

"Deed I do, lady."

"The way you say that makes me think you've been a cowboy. But I never heard a cowboy speak, save in a movie."

"I rode the range from the time I could fork a hawse until I was twenty."

"How interesting! And how soon could you fork a horse?"

"Guess I was close to being born on one and bareback at that. But I was six when I took to herding cattle."

9

"Goodness! Didn't you ever go to school?"

"Yes. I went through high school and had two years — I should say terms — at Normal College in Flagstaff."

"I was wondering how — when you ever got the education you seem to have, if you rode a horse all your life."

"We go to school in winter out heah."

He led Katherine off the main street, to make a detour around a block. It was evident from the noise and smoke that the fire was located on the far side of this square. Katherine had another new sensation — an urge to run to a fire. She was finding unplumbed capacities in herself. The young Westerner, however, was more interesting than the fire. Katherine waited again for him to speak voluntarily. But he did not, nor look at her.

"Your mother is staying at my hotel?" she inquired.

"Yes. I haven't seen her yet. And I shore hate to. . . . I've come to try to stop Mom from divorcing Dad."

"Ah!" Katherine was startled almost to

the point of halting in her tracks. The information frankly volunteered by her escort, given with a poignancy of emotion in sharp contrast to his former reserve, found an instant response in her. This meeting was becoming a more than casual one.

Suddenly it seemed potent. The young Westerner's trouble found an answering chord in her heart. "I'm sorry," went on Katherine, slowly. "This divorce craze! . . . . It's not so very bad though for grown-up children like you — and me."

He did not catch the import of her last words. "It's a craze all right. Not so wrong for young folk like us. But for old people, mother and father, it's daid wrong."

"I agree with you. Oh, I hope you can stop your mother — persuade her to patch it up!"

That expression appeared to hit the young man hard. "I'm afraid you don't know Mom. It'll take an earthquake to shake her. If it was only something else — anything else. . . ."

"Another woman?" interposed Katherine.

"A girl! Only a girl sixteen years old — and a Mexican girl at that," he burst out, as if it relieved him to unburden himself.

"A Mexican senorita! . . . . She'd be pretty, of course?"

"Pretty? Why Marcheta is the prettiest kid that ever bloomed in California. I was sweet on her myself before I got wise to Dad's break. Funny thing! Marcheta liked Dad more than she did me. But then Dad is a grand guy. You'd never guess he is fifty. . . . I don't blame him much for falling for Marcheta. Mom caint or won't understand. . . . I reckon you savvy, ma'am. — It's Dad's only slip, so far as I know. And we've been like brothers. When Mom found out I tried to take the blame. I lied myself blue in the face. But Dad would have none of that. So Mom is heah to divorce Dad. . . . And I reckon we're ruined."

There was a poignant misery in this outburst that entirely disregarded the fact that it was to an entire stranger that such confidences were made. Katherine was quick to understand and respond.

12

"Surely it is not so bad as that. Don't give up," she rejoined, eloquently. "Perhaps I can help you, Mr. Arizona. You and I have something in common."

"What do you mean — ma'am?" he queried, with a catch in his breath. And for the first time he turned to look at her. They had gone around another block. Katherine saw the hotel looming up and beyond it a dark mountain, crowned by white stars. She was in the grip of a swiftly-developing and thought-arresting situation. But her impulse brooked no restraint.

"I am from New York," she said, earnestly. "My mother is here with her boy friend. He is a fortune-hunter. My father — well, he maintained an expensive apartment uptown and spent much time away from home. That gave my mother the chance she was looking for, I fear. She came out here to divorce him and she brought this man with her. If I can't persuade or force her to her senses she will go on with it and marry this person. That will raise a rotten scandal. It will ruin mother."

"Aw! Shore it will. . . . What damn fools these old people are!" ejaculated the young man, with passion. "Your case is worse than mine. It just makes me see red."

"What's your name?" asked Katherine, inspired in spite of an effort to restrain the drift of this interview.

"Phil Cameron."

"Mine is Katherine Hempstead. Let's combine our nerve and our wit. Let's stop our mothers from doing this thing." The words were out before Katherine stopped to consider.

"What! — Why — why — Miss Hempstead," Cameron stammered, blushing like a girl. "You mean for you and I to put our haids together — to help one another — to —"

"Precisely. Two heads are better than one. You are western. I am eastern. We might make a pair to draw to — to use poker lingo. How about it, Arizona?"

They had halted on the corner, under the bright light. Katherine did not flinch under the most searching scrutiny to which she had ever been subjected. But her heart

14

did skip a beat at the look that marked the keen glance of appraisal. It told her that she had more than passed muster.

"It's a great idea, Miss Hempstead," he finally burst out: "What luck for me! I felt so — so sick and blue I wanted to die. How did you ever drop out of the sky like this? It's just wonderful. I cain't believe my eyes and ears. But I say yes, ma'am, bless you! And if it's fighting you need, I'll never fail you."

"I believe it. I'm lucky too. We don't need to inquire into the workings of fate. . . . , shake hands, Phil."

He appeared awkward and under a spell, but his hand left hers paralyzed.

"Oh! — Mr. Arizona, I'll want to use this member again," she said. "Call for me here or give me a ring at nine in the morning. Now let's go in and beard our respective lionesses in their dens."

Chapter 2

On the way to her room Katherine observed that the hotel appeared to be patronized by well-dressed people; there was music and dancing in the dining-room; flowers everywhere, and all the appointments indicated a catering to a cosmopolitan elite.

Katherine telephoned the office from her room and asked for Mrs. Henry Watson Hempstead. The clerk informed her that Mrs. Hempstead was at dinner. Katherine had dined on the train. She took off her coat and hat, all at once aware that she was tired, and that excitement still abided with her. Deciding to put off seeing her mother until next day, Katherine changed her travelling clothes for comfortable pajamas, and sat down to rest and ponder.

She was here in Reno. She had met an interesting young Westerner and had impulsively made a compact with him. The three facts had given rise to a feeling which she could not analyze, except that it was not disagreeable. Katherine got no farther than that in her pondering.

Presently she called Mrs. Hempstead again and received an answer: "Hello. Who is this?" How well Katherine recognized that voice.

"Mother. It's Kay."

"Kay! . . . . Where are you?"

"Here."

"In Reno?"

"Yes. At this hotel."

"My God! . . . . You would. But I never thought you'd follow me. Kay, why in the world did you come?"

"Do you need to ask?"

"Yes, I do. Who told you?"

"Father. He let me read your letter. I had just arrived home from Miami. I didn't even unpack — and here I am."

"Darling, it was adorable of you. But so foolish. That horrible train ride —"

"Was glorious for me, mother. It made me ashamed that I knew so little about my own country. It did something else to me — I don't know what."

"Indeed? How interesting! My eyes were so full of dust I couldn't see out. You like the West, Kay?"

"I believe I will love it."

"You always had different notions from any one else. I'm glad your trip will not be altogether wasted."

Katherine caught the rather broad inference and she replied that she was sure her purpose in coming West would be fulfilled.

"Not if it's what I imagine it is," returned Mrs. Hempstead, with asperity. "Come to my room at once."

"Not tonight, mother. I regret to say that I must give you a very disagreeable few minutes. But I'll put it off until tomorrow. Meanwhile you can think a little over the horrible blunder you have made."

"Kay, I'm breaking all ties," cried

her mother, with emotion.

"You are not doing anything of the kind."

"Kay!" rejoined Mrs. Hempstead, faintly. "Have I ever — interfered with your peculiar ways of being happy?"

"Not lately. For years though you were an unnatural mother. . . . Is your boy friend, Jimmy, here with you?"

"Certainly he's here. Where would he be? . . . . But I detest your vulgarity."

"He ought to be somewhere else, my dearest mother. If you haven't any sense of decency, he ought to have. . . . Does his apartment adjoin yours?"

"Don't insult me, Kay."

"I'll certainly insult him, if that is possible."

"My dear daughter, you seem to be taking a great deal upon yourself. Did you come out alone?"

"Yes, I came alone."

"I rather hoped you'd brought Brelsford. . . . Kay, did you accept him?"

"No."

"Did you refuse him?"

"No."

"But Kay, you will marry him. You must. He's the most eligible and desirable young man you know."

"So you think, mother dea. I like Victor, but marriage. . . . You and father furnish a perfect example of marital felicity, don't you?"

"But Kay, you absolutely must marry. You're twenty-two."

"Quite ancient in fact. That is, I was — until I dropped down here into God's country. I feel very young and romantic — Yes! that's it. I was wondering what ailed me. I've gone back to sixteen, mother. And I think one of these tall sun-browned cowboys will get me."

"Cowboy!" screamed Mrs. Hempstead. "Are you crazy, Kay? You, a Hempstead — with your background — your money! . . . . I'll wire Brelsford to fly out here."

"Don't you dare. *I* don't need anyone to look after me. It's you. . . . But wait, mother darling. That might be a capital idea — sending for Vic. I'd like to see how he'd stack up beside one of these strapping Westerners. . . . Go ahead. Get

Victor out here. It might precipitate things."

"You devil!"

"Good night, mother. I'll see you tomorrow. Sweet dreams."

Katherine turned off the steam heat and opened a window. The desert air blew in, cold, fresh, with a dry tang that was new to her. White stars studded the velvety blue sky. Beyond the narrow border of the town limits stretched a vast space ending in black hills. She gazed a moment, shivering, and then ran to get into bed, grateful for warm blankets.

When she reviewed the conversation with her mother, Katherine felt that she had reason to be encouraged. It had been several months since she had heard her voice. If there was anything she could be sure of, it was her mother's love for her and her sister Polly. That Katherine felt anew, and it softened her scorn and anger. It strengthened the conviction upon which she had dared to come West — that her mother was vulnerable through her one sincere affection. But what course to pursue, Katherine had not yet decided.

Persuasion, argument would be futile. Ridicule and scorn were weapons Mary Hempstead could not endure. She believed in Leroyd's attachment with all a disappointed middle-aged woman's egotism. Probably that would prove ineradicable. Katherine pondered over the problem a while and dismissed it with the decision to let her opposition in this affair rise out of the exigency of future contacts.

Then she fell to pleasant reverie. She recalled the boy with whom she had made the appointment for the morrow. "I like him," she mused to herself. "He just fell perfectly into the picture. Strange how things happen! Was it romance? Did I have a thrill? I — Kay Hempstead? . . . . Yes, I did — and couldn't recognize it. . . . Well, mother, darling, it's an ill wind that blows nobody good. I'm glad at least that your affairs brought me out West."

Upon such thoughts Katherine drifted into sleep. When she awakened golden sunshine shone through the window upon her bed. She saw a wide reach of rolling bronze desert ending in blue-hazed hills.

When had she awakened with such exhilaration? Not in the Alps nor the Adirondacks. And when, scorning the hot water for the cold, she rubbed her cheeks, she found that they would not need any rouge.

The thought uppermost in Katherine's mind was what to wear. Usually such consideration did not dominate her. And she was distinctly amused when she guessed the reason. "That nice Western boy!" she soliloquized. "I wonder would he be flattered if he knew Kay Hempstead desired to look well in his eyes. . . . But he really isn't a boy."

She ordered breakfast to be brought to her room and asked for a maid to unpack her bags and have her clothes pressed. Nine o'clock found her dressed in a new sport suit of violet blue which perfectly matched the color of her eyes. She guessed it must be this invigorating Western air that made her so radiant. Precisely on the dot of nine the telephone rang.

"Hello," answered Katherine.

"Hello. . . . Is this you — Miss — Miss Hempstead?" came the query in a halting

23

voice with a drawl.

"Mawnin', Phil. . . . Yes, this is Miss Hempstead. Kay to her friends."

"Kay?"

"Yes. It's shorter. Not so high-hat."

"May I call you Kay?" he asked, in boyish eagerness.

"I'd like it."

"Thanks. That'll be swell. . . . You asked me to call you at nine. I've been up since five o'clock waiting. Dog-gone! I never knew hours could be so long."

"Are you downstairs?"

"No. At the Elk Hotel. It's a dump about four blocks away."

"Have you a car?"

"Yes. I mean — it was one."

"All right. Call for me at once."

Five minutes later Katherine walked through the lobby, running the gauntlet of staring guests and reporters and agents, out into the brilliant Nevada sunlight. A dilapidated car had just drawn up to the curb. Young Cameron stepped out, bareheaded, a flush on his tanned cheek.

"Howdy Phil," brawled Katherine, and offered her hand.

"Good mawnin'," he returned.

Katherine looked up at him as he shook hands with her. In broad daylight she recalled only his height, his wide shoulders, the glint of his chestnut hair. It did have a curl in it. Gray-blue, piercing eyes shed a glad and incredulous light upon her. Katherine thought he was handsomer than she had remembered.

"Phil, does your Western sun shine this way often?"

"Yes. Every mawnin' about the whole year round. But I reckon it never yet shone on anything so lovely as you."

"What? The language of compliment! And I imagined you a shy tongue-tied Arizona cowboy. . . . Thank you, Phil. You don't distort the general landscape yourself."

"Come round and get in the front seat. . . . I shore have a nerve taking you out in this tin can."

"Don't apologize for your car. It might be a chariot drawn by four white horses. . . . Phil, drive me around the town and out into the country."

"Reno isn't much to see. But the desert

is worth a lot of trouble on a May mawnin'."

Cameron showed her the town, without being able to tell her what was what. Then he drove her out beyond the auto camps, speakeasies and roadhouses and small ranches into the desert. It did not take long to get out of sight of Reno and its environs.

The air was cold, nipping, fragrant, and so dry that Katherine felt it drawing her delicate skin. When she inhaled deeply she felt as if she had drawn of the elixir of life. The desert at close hand seemed to claim some kinship deep within her. Yet it was all wasteland, ridge after rolling ridge, rocks endlessly everywhere, bronze mounds and buttes here, and black walls and lava-fissures there, and all around, in the distance, bold mountains veiled in blue.

"Phil, I have ridden a camel on the Sahara. I've seen the Arabian desert, the lapis-lazuli desert along the Jordan. But they never affected me like this."

"Kay, this is America. This is home. And you ought to see our Arizona desert!

Not like this at all. Heah you see only a two-bit, four-flush bit of outdoors. Why, north of Flagg you can see two hundred miles. Down and down over the gray cedar flats and the grassy range, the yellow bare valley of the Little Colorado, and then up and up over the Painted Desert, the dunes of clay in all colors, the slopes to the escarpments, up to the great red walls that burn into the blue. Oh, I'd love to show you Arizona."

"I'd love to have you. Color is my weakness, Phil. I adore blue. I love red and purple."

"Then you should see our purple sage in bloom."

"Purple sage. I've read of it. . . . Perhaps I'll have you show it to me, if — I mean when we have been successful here with our recalcitrant mothers. Oh, I'd like to ride on and on."

"Kay, can you ride a hawse?"

"I play polo, Mr. Cameron."

"My Gawd, I'd love. . . . Aw, excuse me, Kay. But to see you on a hawse."

"That wouldn't be difficult, if you find the horses. I have my riding togs. . . . Oh!

how splendid! Stop the car here, Phil.''

The road had turned on the edge of a high promontory from which Katherine had a superb view of leagues of desert, where lava cones and black beds led the eye to bleached alkali flats, and on across the land of mirage to the inevitable barriers of mountains. Katherine gazed long at this desolate scene. It approached the sublime in its overpowering starkness. She had never dreamed that the wasteland could affect her like this. It provoked thought, it faced her with herself. Was she really as honest and sincere as she believed herself? What good was she to anybody? Certainly she had not helped materially to make a home for Polly and her mother. All of which restless query and deduction went tumbling through Katherine's consciousness, until a movement on her companion's part brought her back to the present.

"Here I am dreaming when we should be discussing our problem," she said, rousing. "Where shall we begin?"

"I shore don't know. It's got my goat, if you know what I mean," returned

Cameron, in perplexity.

"Did you talk to your mother last night?"

"I should smile I did. I pleaded with her. I used every argument and persuasion in the world. But Mom's as bull-haided as any old cow on the range."

"Naturally, being a wronged woman. But most women do not see clearly. All through the ages they have been wronged — that way. It can't be helped. Religion, morals, education, ties — all these things are lost in the shuffle now and again. A modern woman should recognize that and realize that the lapse may be only temporary. She should bow to what she cannot break."

"Not many girls take such views. I never heard one. I wish you could talk to Mom."

"Perhaps I can, some time. But don't you speak of me. She'd resent it. I'll make her acquaintance before she learns that my mission out here is the same as yours. . . . Phil, it strikes me that if you and I are really going to present an united front in battle against these destroyers of happy homes, we should know more about each other."

"You said you'd risk that walk last night if I would, or something like that. I've gone a long way."

"But don't you want to know anything about me?" asked Katherine in surprise.

"To see you heah is enough."

"Be serious, Phil. Haven't you thought about me at all?"

"I lay awake most of the night — thinking. There's one thing though that — that. . . . Shore, I know you're not married. But are you engaged?"

"No, I'm not. I should tell you, though, that I know a fine chap, Victor Brelsford, whose people have always been close to mine. They all want me to marry him. Mother is rabid on that subject. I haven't been able to make up my mind."

"Well, I should think if you were put on the spot, you'd savvy pronto what was what," declared Cameron, bluntly.

"I didn't. But I do now," she rejoined, thoughtfully. "I never loved Victor. I shall never marry him."

"That's that. I shore feel sorry for

the hombre," said Phil, feelingly.

"Mother threatened she'd wire for Victor to come out West to take care of me. You see I'd confessed my interest in cowboys."

"Aw, don't kid me," implored Cameron, with the blood leaping to his face.

"Phil, I wasn't altogether in fun. To be sure I wanted to upset mother. But I know I'd like cowboys. I like you. I've been used to men too soft, too effete, too civilized, except perhaps in the case of a college football player or two."

"Shore you'd like cowboys. They are the salt of the earth — those I was brought up with. Clean, straight, hard chaps, who'd fight and shoot too, as quick as that."

"Shoot! In this modern day? You mean in the movies, Phil?"

"Well, I've been off the range for some years, worse luck. All the same that holds good. . . . I'm shore proud you like me, Kay. I'll try to deserve it."

"Boy, you're taking me for granted. Face value, you know, is risky. But I want to know more about you."

"Okay with me. Just ask?"

"This first one is funny. Are you married?"

"Good Lord — no!"

"Well, perhaps you're engaged? Girls, even in California must be like those I know."

"I'm not engaged," replied Phil, soberly.

"But you must have lots of girls?"

"Why must I?"

"Never mind. But have you?"

"I'd shore like to lie and say I had. Only the fact is I haven't a single darn girl."

"What a terrific waste of good looks and sterling young manhood!" rejoined Katherine flippantly. Then more seriously, "But I'm glad, Phil. It wouldn't be so good if you were. Your lady-love would come over here and upset our applecart.... How old are you, Phil?"

"I feel fifteen this mawnin', but I'm twenty-six. . . . No boy any more, as Mom said."

"You adore her, don't you?"

"I reckon."

"You work, of course. I felt your hand. It was as rough almost as sandpaper. But what kind of work?"

"All kinds, believe me. My job is to superintend Dad's ranch. He has a thousand acres in grapes and a couple of hundred in oranges. Dad employs a good many Mexicans. Our ranch is one of the biggest in Southern California. Near Redlands. At this season you can see orange blossoms and oranges, and right above them the mountains white with snow."

"How beautiful! I've read of that, too. And to think I've never seen California."

"If you ever come, *I* want to show it to you."

"That's a promise. I'll come, Phil."

"Too good to ever come true! . . . But I mustn't forget about my ranch. An aunt left me some money a couple of years ago. I blew ten thousand of it for a mile square of land down in the Coachella Valley near the Salton Sea. It's way below sea-level there. Hell in summer. Dad swore I was crazy. But I developed water — two dandy

33

artesian wells. Hot water. I irrigated and put in dates and grapefruit. The fellow I have in charge made fourteen thousand dollars on five acres of grapefruit on his place adjoining last year. Well, my vineyard and orchard spring up over night, almost. Just grew grand. You see, after all, the land didn't have any alkali. I'd picked a winner. I had a gold mine. Then the depression hit the coast. Dad almost went under. He couldn't help me. I'm deep in debt now, and if I cain't get a loan, a mortgage on my ranch I'm going to lose it. Aw, but that will be tough!"

"Loan? How much will you need, Phil?" she asked, quietly.

"Not so much, I reckon. Only a few thousand to save the ranch. But where'n h — heck can a fellow get a loan these days? The banks are no good. They're crooked. . . . Aw, if I had fifteen or twenty thousand dollars to develop my ranch in five years I'd be drawing down that much a year profit."

"Phil, would it make you sick to hear that I spend that much on my clothes alone, every year?"

"My Gawd! — You don't say? . . . .
Kay, you don't need so many clothes.
They cain't make you any lovelier."

"More compliment! Can't we be
serious? . . . . I guess I know all I want to
about you. . . . And now to our problem.
What to do with our mothers. Mine is the
limit. She's nutty. Thinks she is in love.
Thinks she's young still and adored for
herself. She's furious with my father. She
will be with me. She's stubborn. She's
strong-willed. What can we do with a
woman like that?"

"You said the hombre she brought out
is a fortune-hunter?"

"I know it. I knew that before I was
told. Leroyd is a gambler, too."

"He'll get cleaned proper out heah,
believe me. Does she know he's a
gambler?"

"Probably not. She has lent him
money, though. My banker told me."

"Kay, I'll sort of trail that gent up in
good old Arizona fashion. *Quien sabe?* I
might get something on him. . . . I'm
getting a hunch that my case with Mom is
hopeless, unless I can scare her."

"Scare her? — Phil, you don't mean physically?"

"No. About me, I mean. I've got a hunch I must do something terrible."

"On her account!" exclaimed Katherine, breathlessly.

"Shore."

She clasped his arm tightly and looked up into his eyes, unmindful of the effect upon him. "Phil! You're a darling. You're a genius! You've hit it — plumb center. I, too, must do something terrible. I must scare my mother out of her wits. I am her weakness — the same as you are your mother's. But what to do — how — how?"

"Kay, do you take — spells like this often?" asked Phil, huskily.

"Spells! I never had one before," replied Katherine, innocently enough. She had not intended to practice any charm of glance or word or person upon him. But the havoc had been wrought. Katherine could not be sorry. As she drew away she felt an unusual warmth creep from neck to cheek. "Phil, I'll probably have more of them — spells, I mean," she went on,

36

joyously. "It's just marvelous — my coming West — this intrigue we're involved in — the outwitting of our mothers — the romance of it!"

"Yeah? Well, it's marvelous, all right. And I'll be game. But it's my finish, Kay!"

Chapter 3

Late in the afternoon of that day Katherine sought her mother. She had deliberately refrained from an earlier meeting because she had found, on previous occasions, that the longer her mother waited the more amenable she became. Mrs. Hempstead was a nervous, imperious, high-strung woman, more governed by emotion than by reason. Katherine entered the room with her usual cool poise, and for the first time in her life she omitted to kiss this parent. It was an omission that apparently stung.

"Well, Mrs. Henry Watson Hempstead, here I am."

"So I observe. It took you a long time.

I've waited all day."

"Now that I've gotten here, I'll make my appeal short and to the point."

"Appeal? — Oh, Kay! You insulted me last night. . . . You freeze me today. I'm your mother. I'm not an old woman, nor a stone. Have you no feeling?"

"I am conscious of a great deal of feeling. But how much of it is sympathy with your mad project will appear presently."

"Kay, how stunning you look!" exclaimed Mrs. Hempstead, as if impelled against her will. "I never saw you look so wonderful!"

"Thanks, mother. You can lay it to this glorious West. I've got the desert air in my lungs — the sun in my blood. . . . Forgive me if I fail to return the compliment in any measure. You don't look so well."

Mrs. Hempstead's pale worn face flushed. She looked all of her forty-eight years. Her make-up failed to hide a pallor of lassitude. She was still handsome, but there was a shadow, a blight of worry and strain on her face.

Katherine became prey to a suspicion that had not before beset her in her brooding. It rankled. It motivated against the love and pity she still had in goodly measure. Nevertheless her sense of tolerance and justice, her own outlook on life, rebuked her with the thought that her mother had a right to love. On the moment, but for one single fact, Katherine would have made friends with her mother and have abandoned her resolve to prevent the divorce. If Jimmy Leroyd had not been a ruined man about town, a spendthrift and a fortune-hunter, Katherine would have surrendered gracefully and have sanctioned the affair. But she knew Leroyd. She sensed here that the intimacy between him and her mother had gone far. Such a thing was as common in her set as conversation over the breakfast table. But coming at last close to her own home, it sickened Katherine a little and steeled her nerve.

"How far have you gone with your divorce proceedings?" queried Katherine, abruptly, as she sat down opposite Mrs. Hempstead's reclining chair.

"I haven't engaged my lawyer yet. They ask too much. Twenty-five hundred dollars seems excessive to pay — even for desirable freedom."

"You can get your divorce for two hundred and fifty," returned Katherine, brusquely. "If you must go through with it, don't let them rob you. That's far too much to pay for Jimmy Leroyd."

"Don't be catty, Kay. . . . Let me tell you once for all, I — I must go through with it."

"Nevertheless, mother darling, I will have my say, as a dutiful daughter. . . . Father is sorry. He told me he thought you knew — that you just wanted an excuse you didn't need. He would not have opposed your friendship with Leroyd. But to go to extremes — to divorce him — that cut father deeply. He cannot see any sense in it. Neither can I."

"I want my freedom," protested Mrs. Hempstead. "I never loved Henry. It was my mother's match."

"Like your obsession to give me to Brelsford," murmured Katherine. "It's a fine world to live in — if you don't weaken. . . . Mother, it's not true that you never cared for father. I know better than that."

"Kay, I — I — care a great deal for Jimmy Leroyd."

"I confess there must be something," rejoined Katherine with a calculated brutality. "You're a sentimental old woman."

"I am not — at least not old," cried her mother, cruelly hurt.

"Listen, mother, before I lose my temper and tell you what you don't know. Never mind father. And leave me out of your consideration. But think of Polly. She loves you — far more than you deserve. She loves father, too. It'll be rotten of you to turn her over to the ranks of children without mothers. Polly is fine, sweet, deep. She has brains and soul. If you do this absurd thing it will absolutely damn that child — wreck her life."

"Does she — know yet?" asked Mrs. Hempstead, in a suffocated voice.

"No. Father didn't tell her. But if you persist I must tell her."

"She will get over it," said the

mother, breathing hard.

"You force me to be brutal," returned Katherine, with cold scorn, as she arose. "I see that you have lost all sense of responsibility. You are conscienceless. Your fortune-hunting gambler has made you lose all sense of proportion and decency, has enmeshed you in a middle-aged love affair that makes you ridiculous."

"Say your worst, Kay. You always had a two-edged tongue. But you — can't change me," whispered Mrs. Hempstead, looking as if she were on the point of collapse.

"I've lost my desire to," returned Kay, bitterly. "Go to hell in your own way. I'll go in mine."

"You'll — what?" cried her mother hoarsely, revived as by a lash on a raw wound.

"I'll dispense with a lot of my ideas on the subject of decency. A fine example you give me to marry. My God! the idea turns my stomach. . . . Father will take Polly. That leaves me free. The Hempsteads are done. What do I care?" The scorn and bitterness that Kay managed to inject into her voice was not all acting.

"But my daughter! . . . . You have Brelsford. He adores you. He can save your name, at least. For heaven's sake don't let my — my affair ruin you."

"Victor is probably all any woman might want. But I don't love him. I won't marry him."

"Oh, Kay! — You've decided that?"

"Yes."

"Since you came West?"

"Yes."

"Mercy! You'll be the death of me. Have you forgotten — your position — your wealth — your duty to your class?"

"Almost, thank God. After all, such things don't amount to anything in this country out here."

"This country! This wilderness of dust and wind? These sordid little towns — these crude people? You couldn't live here?"

"Why couldn't I? I'm sick of that idle deceitful world. I'd love some dust and wind in my face. I have begun to believe these Westerners you call crude are fine, simple, honest, true. True! They work. . . .

I think I'll go in the movies."

Mrs. Hempstead screamed and sank back almost fainting. Katherine's random shot seemed to her mother a terrible threat.

In the hall outside, Katherine encountered Leroyd. He appeared younger, more debonair than when she had met him last some months ago. Well-groomed, handsome in his fair way, a man of good family, Leroyd looked more than ever the cavalier for such idle and unsatisfied women as Mrs. Hempstead. He greeted Katherine in his smooth manner, not in the least concerned by the intent look she bestowed upon him.

"Lovelier than ever, Kay. It's great to see you," he added.

"Jimmy, I've had it out with mother," replied Katherine, peremptorily. "You will please give me a few minutes of your valuable time."

"Delighted, I'm sure. Where shall we proceed to the execution?"

"There's a sitting-room on this floor."

"Will you smoke? A Lucky might soothe your ruffled nerves."

Katherine declined with thanks and led

him to the far end of the corridor, where an intimate little lounge opened upon a balcony above spacious gardens. But she did not go outside. Kay sat down and motioned him to a seat beside her.

"Jimmy, I came West to try to persuade mother not to sue for a divorce," began Katherine, deliberately. "She refused."

"I fear yours are vain oblations, my dear Kay."

"Indeed they are. But it just struck me that you might not be so difficult."

"How flattering! Go on."

"Jimmy, you have taken money from my mother. I have found out. A considerable sum, altogether."

"Certainly. I borrowed it," replied Leroyd, blandly, but the red came up in his face.

"Permit me to be slangy," retorted Kay, flippantly. "Baloney to that. You never intended to pay it back. You never will. Jimmy, you're not the kind of gambler who pays."

"Gambler? You are disposed to be facetious," he said not so imperturbably as before.

"I mean what I say. I had you looked up, Jimmy. And in further parlance of the age, I have your number. . . . What'll you take in cold cash to ditch my mother?"

"Kay, you surprise me — not to say more."

"Would you take a hundred thousand dollars?"

"No," he replied.

"That's my limit. . . . Has it occurred to you, Jimmy, that I could take you away from mother, if I wanted to?"

"It has not. What an enchanting prospect."

"You know I could do it?"

"Kay, a denial of that would be absurd. You could take any man away from any woman."

"You're not worth what it'd cost. Nor is mother worth it. Nor is father. But poor Polly!"

"Kay, I swear I love that child as dearly as if she were my own," declared Leroyd, with indubitable sincerity.

"Your one saving grace, Jimmy. But who could help loving that exquisite little girl? . . . . Well, there doesn't seem to be

any more to say. There isn't any more —
to you."

"I'm sorry, Kay. I bear you no
resentment. Really. But I'm devoted to
your mother. And that's that. . . . I advise
you to go back home."

"Not much. I'm going to paint this
Reno the most beautiful flaming red that
it ever saw."

"Kay! You're not serious?" he
expostulated in consternation, his languid
eyes starting and his jaw dropping.

"I was serious. Now I will be gay."

"But your mother could not stand your
— such notoriety — here in the limelight.
Good God!"

"I'll wash my hands of her. Go your
dirty ways, both of you."

"Kay!"

But Katherine was sweeping down the
corridor, her head high, with bells of
inspiration and triumph in her ears.

Not until the following day did
opportunity arise for Katherine to make
the acquaintance of Phil Cameron's
mother. Then, as luck decreed, it came
about naturally and without the slightest

apparent design on her part.

She found Mrs. Cameron a comely woman somewhat over fifty with a lined sweet face upon which was written a record of the years of hard western life. She had been handsome once. Katherine traced some resemblance to Phil in her features. A few minutes of casual conversation were sufficient for Katherine to discern the woman's simplicity, that she was as transparent as an inch of crystal water. That was long enough, too, to divine that her heart was almost broken. Katherine experienced a warm rush of emotion at the thought that this was Phil's mother and that she might help her.

Mrs. Cameron, evidently, in this crisis of her life, was not proof against sympathy, and the evident interest Katherine did not need to pretend. The distracted mother and wronged wife wanted to unburden herself. She needed a woman to confide in. Fate had it in the fact that, with a hotel full of women from all over the United States, society women, business women, motion picture stars and stage actresses, all wronged or unsatisfied or dissatisfied wives seeking freedom from their fetters, Katherine should be the one to draw lovely unhappy Mary Cameron.

"What are *you* here for, Miss — Miss Wales, I think the clerk said was your name?" asked Mrs. Cameron, earnestly, on the full tide of her yearning to unburden herself, yet dubious about this brilliant girl who appeared so kindly.

"Hilda Wales. But that's not my real name. I'll tell you my story sometime. Oh, such a miserable story! I hate to think of it."

"But you're so young! . . . . You don't wear a wedding ring. So you cain't be heah to — for the same reason all these poor women are."

"Including you, Mrs. Cameron?"

"Alas, too true! I came to divorce my husband."

"Ah, I'm so sorry. What is wrong? Don't you care for him? . . . Forgive me. That just popped out. I can see whatever the trouble is, it's not your fault."

Then briefly the sordid little drama, as old and bitter as life, yet different because of the anguish and intimacy of the sufferer, unfolded itself to Katherine's ears. She replied as earnestly and simply as she knew how, intensely relieved and glad that she could be honestly sorry. There could be only one reason in the world why Phil Cameron's father could wound so mortally the woman who had grown up with him, fought the desert and the battle of life beside him; and then because nature is crueller than life, had faded and lost her bloom, her youth, her response. The blame and the wrong, if there were one, could not be laid to Mary Cameron; and viewed with the wisdom and understanding of modern thought, hardly upon Frank Cameron.

Katherine asked a number of simple questions, easy for the troubled woman to answer, the last of which brought the scarlet to her livid cheek.

"Does he want you to divorce him?"

"Oh, dear no. All Frank wanted was to keep me from finding out. He could never manage that ranch without me."

"Mrs. Cameron, I — I wonder if you are doing right."

"That's just what Phil said," flashed

the mother, showing that she still had spirit and fire. "You young folks are all alike. Naturally, of course. I'm old-fashioned, I know. But so Frank ought to be."

"Phil, your son, tell me about him," suggested Katherine. She desired to hear this boy's praises sung by his mother.

They were sung in full measure, and Katherine reflected that if Phil were worthy of them he was a paragon among mothers' only sons.

"Phil is heah at Reno now," went on Mrs. Cameron. "He came to stop me from getting the divorce. We quarreled last night. He didn't come to see me this mawnin'. . . . Phil didn't take Frank's part, Miss Wales. Don't misjudge him. Why, he knocked his father flat for. . . . You see Frank was furious and he swore at me — slapped my face. I reckon I — I was some sharp. But I was jealous of that black-eyed little hussy. *Jealous!* — There, it's out, and it'll do me good. Marcheta is the prettiest girl in Southern California. . . . Well, Phil cain't see my side. And I cain't see his."

"Tell me Phil's side, Mrs. Cameron."

"Oh, it kept me awake all night," replied the mother in distress. "I know I'm old and out of date. But I cain't help my feelings. Phil says I'm wrong. That I should never have let on I knew. That if there was anything wrong it was Frank and me marrying when we were the same age. Because only for so long was I able to be Frank's mate! He didn't say wife or comrade. He just said mate, as if I was some kind of an animal. . . . Oh, it was terrible to heah Phil say such things. I felt like the world had gone on leaving me out, which it has! Then he softened it all by saying this — this thing would peter out of its own accord. Marcheta would marry some young buck and everything would be all right again. But I *cain't* see that. I'll never get over it. I — I want to make Frank suffer."

"Being a woman, I'm on your side," returned Katherine. "But Phil is right. The bitter fact is one of evolution, not right or wrong."

"That may all be true. I don't understand it, and I don't care," replied

Mrs. Cameron, stubbornly.

"Have you thought that you might lose your son by this step?"

"Oh, never! — My son! *Phil?* He would not desert me," cried the little woman, in poignant anguish.

"He might. If he's such a wonderful boy, I wouldn't risk it. I can tell he's modern. If I were you, Mrs. Cameron, I'd settle this vexatious question on one score only. I'd let my decision depend on what it did to my son."

"Decision! — I've sued my husband for a divorce. The case will come up presently. It's too late, even if — if —"

"You can withdraw your suit."

"I won't do it."

"But suppose this home-breaking course of yours threatens to ruin your son?" asked Katherine, launching her last and strongest shaft.

It struck home. Of all catastrophes, Mrs. Cameron had never imagined such a one. She was shocked. Doubt and fear added their dark shadows to her sad face. Katherine's heart ached for her. Yet it was singing, too, for she saw sure victory for

Phil in his mother's love. Through that she could be won or driven.

And on the moment Phil entered the hotel reception room, hat in hand, his striking face and form instinct with vivid life. He gave a start at sight of Katherine with his mother, then he came up to them, smiling, his eyes like blue flames.

"Mom Cameron! — How'd you meet my girl friend?"

"Phil, do you — know Miss Wales?"

"I'm happy to say I do."

"But you said a Miss Hemp — something or other," faltered his mother.

Katherine rose, to give Phil a significant glance of hope, of assurance.

"I have a number of names, Mrs. Cameron," she said, with a laugh. "Mrs. Hempstead is my last. I'm here to divorce my third husband. Hilda Wales is my screen name. I'm a motion picture actress. . . . We'll talk again about this miserable divorce business. For me, though, it's good publicity. . . . I'm awfully happy to find you Phil's mother. We must be great friends."

Then ignoring the utter consternation in

Mrs. Cameron's countenance, she faced Phil, finding him pale, stern, yet with a fascinated understanding.

"Phil darling, don't forget our heavy date tonight. Formal. But we're painting the town red."

Chapter 4

That Phil Cameron would fall in love with her had been a foregone conclusion to Katherine. Not egotism but experience had taught her that this was almost inevitable. Propinquity with her seemed to have but one result. As a girl up to eighteen she had been sorry over many a boy's heartbreak, and had excessively grieved herself more than once. As a woman she had learned that men desired her kisses while they were deaf to her thoughts. That had not made her callous. But it had encased her in a mocking unattainable shell, through which men, with the perversity of masculine nature, tried only the harder to break.

But Katherine knew, not quite at first, but soon, that she was different with Phil. It was the complex situation, the intense resolve to circumvent her mother, the frank manliness of this western boy, and a revolt in herself that seemed to be the influence of the desert — these were the factors which were apparently placing her restrained past farther and farther behind her.

The plot she had concocted to defeat her mother's aims, which she was convinced would succeed equally well in the case of Mrs. Cameron, she had not yet entirely disclosed to Phil. During these few glamorous days she grew to know him better. He would have to be terribly in love with her before he would consent to her plan. And there was something inexplicably sweet in helping this along by all the honest charms and wiles of women. When Phil protested that they were letting the hours slide by, doing nothing, while the divorce proceedings were working toward fruition, she merely smiled and bade him wait.

Katherine had no difficulty, however, in

contriving to keep Phil with her from early morning until late at night. They drove all over the desert, which she particularly loved, gambled in the casinos, went to the movies, dressed and dined and danced at the hotels, all the time avoiding their mothers as much as possible. To Katherine's delight this procedure had begun to annoy and perplex Mrs. Hempstead, as it had distressed Mrs. Cameron. The former saw her darling flirting with a common cowboy and the latter saw her darling in the clutches of a beautiful siren from Hollywood. If Phil had not been so worried, he, too, would have been gleeful over this mental state of the two mothers.

In Phil's case Kay discerned that it was going to require more than propinquity. He was western. He had been brought up in the open country. He had been taught respect for women. He was tremendously proud that Kay chose to spend all her time with him, that she never so much as met the eyes of other men. Her beauty dazzled him. He had fallen in love with her from the first. He knew it and had no regrets.

But so far, he had not even permitted himself to imagine a closer relation. Kay was a gorgeous creature from another and different world from his. The boyish homage he accorded her was fit for a princess. But to possess her he did not even dream of.

"He's the finest cleanest man I ever knew," mused Kay, before her mirror that night, as she proceeded with an exquisite toilet. "I'm falling in love with Phil — and I'm glad. It's like my few cases when I was sixteen, only worse. It'll make easier what I must do. . . . But afterward — Oh, dear!"

And at that stage of soliloquy Kay studied her image in the mirror. It was not to satisfy her vanity or to draw pleasure from that beautiful reflection. She suddenly felt that she saw another and different Kay Hempstead. The golden hair that crowned her head, the broad low brow, the serious violet eyes, the curved red lips — these she had gazed at innumerable times, but never as now. She imagined there was a new spirit actuating her.

"I will *not* think. Sufficient unto the day!" she said, and in those deliberate words crossed her Rubicon.

That evening at dinner in the spacious dining room of the Reno, Katherine had eyes for no one but Phil. When they danced she dropped that instinctive bar which she had always placed between her and her partners. She slipped her hand far up around Phil's shoulder and leaned to him so close that she felt the pounding of his heart. Immediately her own became unruly.

From that time on Katherine drifted into perilous ways with her eyes wide open. Deliberately she exercised all the arts of coquetry. She gave royally of her smiles, her glances, her laughter and whisper, of the beauty and lure of her person. But such dangerous tactics, though they awakened in Phil all she wanted, reacted with irresistible rebound upon herself. This she deserved, this she made light of, this she hoped would last long and hurt deeply, though the worldly cynicism in her wild scornful doubts. Nevertheless she forgot the fleeting of the days, and almost the vital reason for her sojourn in Nevada.

One night when the moon was full she persuaded Phil to drive her out on the desert, to the promontory which had become her favorite place. With furs around her bare arms and shoulders she leaned silently against him, conscious that the critical hour had come. That, or the mystic and profound splendor of the desert by night, somehow saddened her into reticence. The dark gulf of the Mediterranean, the Vale of Cashmir, the Valley of Yumuri, none of the voids in the earth that she had viewed from heights, had ever had power to affect her as this naked rent in the desert, lonely, fierce, primitive as ever back in the ages that had formed it. Again she felt that this primal thing had much to do with the influence the West had upon her. Desert and elements, the men out here were far closer to the primitive than all she had known in the east and abroad. They had awakened a response in her heart. And some day there would come a reckoning and a choice.

"Have you ever seen anything more

wonderful than this desert in the moonlight?" she asked, presently.

"Yes, Kay," he replied, with an unsteady note in his voice, "you!"

"But you haven't looked at the desert under the moon," she complained.

"How can I?"

"Oh. . . . Then you like how I look tonight?"

"Kay, I haven't caught my breath yet. . . . Aw, what luck for me to be with you — to dance with you — hold . . . to see you so many different ways, each one lovelier than the last!"

"Good luck or bad luck?"

"Good, Kay. Wonderful luck! Something to sustain me — when you go back home."

"Then you'll not be unhappy?"

"I cain't swear that, though my whole life should be a paradise of memory."

"Phil, do you love me?"

"Do you need to ask? Doesn't every person in Reno, almost, know that I'm mad about you? Didn't Mom accuse me of being the playboy of a movie-queen?"

"Nevertheless, I do ask."

He uttered a short laugh. "Kay, I love you so well it's heaven to be with you — hell to be away from you. No man was ever so uplifted, so happy."

"Phil! . . . So well? Yet, my boy, you have never asked me for anything. And your one wild break was to hold my hand in the dark movie theatre!"

He was too sincere, too terribly in earnest to see anything strange in her surprise or the import of her statements, and he let them pass unanswered.

"Time is flying, Phil. And we have done so little to block these divorce proceedings," said Kay, at last reverting to the issue at hand.

"Aw, I get sick when I think of that," replied Cameron, feelingly. "I just hate to see Mom. She won't give in. She's more set than ever. And when I do see her, she raves so about you that I rush right away. Kay, I wish you'd let me correct that idea you gave her — that you were a much-divorced movie girl."

"Not yet. It was an inspiration. Phil, my mother moans about my affair with you. 'That strapping cowpuncher! Why he might kidnap you and pack you off to the desert'. . . . When I told her I hoped you would she nearly had hysterics. . . . If we could only see the humor of this situation!"

"Humor? Huh, it's about as funny as being rolled on by a hawse."

"Phil, I've solved our problem," declared Kay, solemnly. "I've found out how to bring my mother and your mother to their knees."

"For Pete's sake, spring it on me."

Kay felt the need of a deep full breath. It was not so easy to make a perfectly atrocious, deliberately abnormal proposition to this clear-eyed, clean-minded young westerner who worshipped her and held her little less than an angel. But the exigency of the case justified such an appalling plot as she had conceived. Already she had devoted days and nights of thinking and feeling toward that end.

"Listen — Phil," she began, haltingly. "And hear me through before you break over the traces. . . . There is only one way to change our mothers. That is to justify the dread they already have. We must scare them to death. Ruthlessly. Mother loves me. Your mother adores you. They live in us, if they only knew it. If they could be shown that you and I were going 'plumb to hell,' as you call it — that their disregard of children's rights and loves had ruined us, made us bitter, reckless, *bad* — they would be horribly upset. They would weaken. They would give up this divorce proceeding. Well, let's do it. That is, let's *pretend* to go to the bad. We'll rent a cottage. I already have one picked out! . . . Don't look at me like that, Phil Cameron. I *have*. You'll say it's swell. We'll have the car I've hired. . . . We'll move into this cottage, bag and baggage, unmarried, brazen as brazen can be. Then we'll cut loose to scandalize even Reno. We'll bet the roof off these gambling places. We'll mop up hard liquor, apparently, in sight of the high and low of this town. We'll make them think that we have thrown decency to the winds — that my mother's disgusting affair and your mother's hard and narrow creed have opened our eyes to the bald realism of life. We're sick of it all. We'll have no more of it. We'll take the fleshpots of

Egypt and to hell with the rest. . . .

"There, Phil! — That's my plan. Whatever you think — you can't say it's not original. Come. Don't slay me — with your eyes!"

It had been his piercing gaze that made Kay falter at the close. She had expected anything but cool stern composure.

"My God! — You're a wonder. The nerve of you! . . . . Kay, it's a swell idea. It's great. But I cain't see it your way."

"Do you think it'd work?" she queried.

"Shore it would. Absolutely. Mom just couldn't see my falling that way on her account. And that stuck-up mother of yours would fall like a ton of bricks. They'd be knocked out, Kay."

"You are sure, Phil? From your man's viewpoint?"

"Yes. It'd work. Pity we cain't floor them. But we just cain't, Kay."

"Why not?" began Katherine, gathering strength with the rebellious query.

"It'd ruin you — disgrace you."

"Boy, we'd only pretend. We'd play a game — a great game. Be actors. All for a good purpose. Oh, the idea thrills me!"

"But the harm would be done, darling. No matter where you went afterward there'd be some dirty hombre or some catty woman bobbing up to tell it."

"Let the future take care of itself," retorted Kay, enigmatically. "We must win this game. I tell you that even if we really went to the bad . . . it'd be worth it to save little Polly's love for her mother and save your mother from a lonely miserable old age."

"I get you, Steve," returned Phil, hoarsely. "But I happen to love you — and your honor — more than the good you name."

"Won't you do it, Phil?" entreated Kay.

"I shore won't."

"Please . . . darling."

"No, by God!"

"We could correct — all the slander, the misunderstanding — somehow — later."

"Even if we could — which I shore doubt —"

"Phil, wouldn't it mean anything, if you really love me, to have me alone that way — seeing me at all hours — and everyway — trusting you where I would trust no other man on earth?''

''Yes. I reckon it'd mean a hell of a lot,'' burst out Phil, his eyes flaming. ''But I'm damned if I'll give these men heah — that you wouldn't wipe your little shoes on — a chance to point the finger of shame at you.''

''Why, you child, what do *I* care for the opinions of men. I'd never see them point — never hear them speak. I am aloof from all that.''

''Kay, it — it hurts me to see you so daid set on this,'' rejoined Phil, hurriedly. ''I never reckoned I could refuse you anything. Aw, you're putting me in a tough spot.''

''Yes. But it's for me.'' She threw wide the furs that enveloped her, and turning, lay back in his arms. The moonlight shone upon her golden head, upon her white face upturned to his, appealingly, upon her lovely neck and breast. ''Phil, don't let me fail in this. I give you my word — I'll pay whatever it costs.''

''Kay, you're talking wild,'' he

said, hoarsely.

"You're the dearest boy I ever knew," she rejoined, dreamily.

"Boy? I reckon — and pretty callow at that."

She lay there gazing up at him, conscious of an emotion which she took for happiness at being in his arms, mocking herself with the thought that it was only stooping to gain her end.

"Kiss me, Phil," she whispered, presently.

"*Kay!* .... You .... Aw, it's only you want your way," he cried, in torment.

"Suppose it is. I ask you. Here I am in your arms. I must care — something . . . or I wouldn't want to. . . ."

Cameron wrenched his powerful shoulders in his effort to resist, yet they were bending closer over her all the time. He was so blind that his lips did not at first find hers. When they did, they merged a boy's soul into a man's passion. Kay felt suffocating in that embrace. But the response she gave, which her sincerity made her think was the least she could do, rewarded her with the sweetest sensation of her whole life, and then flooded her heart with sadness over a hollow victory. He was won. But then her conscience flayed her.

Next day Katherine and Phil moved into the cottage she had chosen. It was one block from the center of town, directly across, with several other cottages, from Reno's second large and fashionable hotel. It sat back among green shrubbery quite isolated, but the gravel driveway and the path were open to idle curious eyes. It had been newly decorated and furnished, and contained one bedroom with bath, a living room, a kitchen and a small room for a servant. Kay had to put part of her baggage in the living room. She assured the dubious Phil that to dispense for once with maid and luxury would be a very good experience for her and one she expected to enjoy because of its novelty.

When they had established themselves, Kay and Phil sat down deliberately to plan their campaign of deviltry. Whatever had been Phil's scruples and pangs they were gone, or hidden under a rapt reckless cowboy's exterior. Kay could not doubt that he was in a transport. She could not probe his thought as to the future, after this debacle. She feared he had burned his bridges behind him and that the future beyond was blank. It did not take long for their quick wit to shape events.

Phil made off down street to purchase cowboy garb, to ingratiate himself into the good graces of the press reporters, to make friends with the chief of police, whom he already knew.

Kay drove to the Hotel Reno and the opening shot fired in the battle was to snub her mother deliberately in front of guests who knew Kay's relation to her. Leroyd she passed with an icy stare. When Mrs. Hempstead could not hide the sting of a cut, it was pretty deep. Well satisfied with this start Kay sat down to wait for Phil and to think about him. Actually the grave side of this drama had reverted to this western boy. Kay had made no other acquaintances and her part was to be absolutely oblivious to her surroundings. An expert in the art of make-up, she was to strive for as tragic and lost an appearance as possible, and to act accordingly.

At last Phil strode in, somehow different, though spurs and boots and belt with empty gunsheath, and a huge sombrero in his hand scarcely accounted for the change. He looked the true range-man, splendid, lithe, hard, and the shyness, the diffidence that had marked his demeanor were gone. It struck Kay that Phil was not an actor. He was being himself.

"Howdy, honey," he called, loud enough for nearby watchers to hear. "What do you know about this?"

He laid an open letter upon Kay's lap. It was a notification from a Desert Bank of Indio, California, that there was a balance of twenty-five thousand dollars there to his account.

"Oh, that? I'd forgotten," she replied, with a smile, as she handed it back. "I notified my banker in New York to forward this amount. Just a loan, Phil — or an interest in your ranch, as you like."

His eyes were beautiful to see and terrible to look into. He bent over to whisper: "Kay, what good will saving my ranch do — if I die of love?"

"Boy, that never kills."

"Quien sabe? . . . . Come on, beautiful, let's go tear things."

Kay drove the big white car with such speed, and apparent recklessness, that a traffic officer caught up with them, and presented them with a ticket. Phil gave the officer such a berating that a crowd gathered. After that incident, they ran the gamut of the more pretentious gambling halls. To all appearances they had been drinking. In places frequented by all classes of people, where nothing save a big wager or a fight ever caused gamblers and spectators to turn away from the games, Phil and Kay created a sensation. He looked like a handsome motion picture cowboy, enamored of his companion. Kay knew she could play a part, and hers was that of a wealthy Easterner with a passion to gamble, to whom money was as the dust under her feet. A crowd followed them from table to table. Phil lost more than he won. But Kay could not lose and her wagers were as large as the games permitted.

That night, Katherine, resplendent and patrician in white, blazing with jewels, walked with Phil into the fashionable dining room of the Reno, timing her advent to her mother's dinner hour. It so happened that Mrs. Hempstead had guests that evening. The head waiter generously bribed by Kay beforehand, had reserved a table close to her mother's. Kay might not have known her mother was alive, so oblivious did she appear to all save this stalwart cowboy, pale, fire-eyed, by far the handsomest man in a room full of handsome men.

They were the cynosure of all eyes. They must have been the despair of Kay's mother, and the little drab woman who sat in a far corner, fascinated as by a snake, clasping and unclasping her hands. Like all cowboys, Phil could stand a few drinks of hard liquor. But this night they had champagne. It went to Phil's head. To Kay's delight and intense gratification he transgressed all the laws of etiquette, as well as decorum. Phil simply overplayed his part. But Kay felt sure she was perfect in hers — that of a disillusioned woman to whom the world was dross, who knew her class to be rank with hypocrisy, who had chosen a primitive cowboy to be her dissolute consort.

Before the dinner was half finished Mrs. Hempstead, suffering from horror and shock, had to be escorted from the dining room.

"How'm I doin', Kay?" quoth Phil, gayly. "Did you get a peep at your old lady as they were packing her off?"

"Yes, I saw her, and I'm divided between joy and sorrow," replied Kay. "You're going fine. In fact you're very natural. You're not over-acting at all. Don't drink any more champagne."

"All right. We've shot the works. Let's dance once more — then go back to our hogan."

"Hogan?" queried Kay, as he rose.

"Darling, a hogan is Indian for domicile, wigwam, shack, cabin, home, or what have you."

"You show your Indian tonight, Phil, more than in language. But as Polly would say — 'I think you're just grand!' . . . . Oh, where will this end?"

"Don't lose your nerve," returned Phil, sternly. "You're the spirit of this deal. We're in it. We got it half won now. . . . Let's cut the dance. . . . My God! Get a look at *my* mother's face."

Chapter 5

Every morning Katherine drove out into the desert with Phil, where they could be themselves for a few hours. Kay forgot her mother then and addressed herself to her own increasing problem, which confronted her in each thoughtful hour. If this stark and rugged Nevada affected her so powerfully, what would golden California be like, and especially purple-saged, canyon-walled Arizona? Kay could only guess at it and revel in her intention to see for herself. At the least, she meant to stay a very good while out west, and if she still maintained a home in New York, on which question she was dubious, she would come back west again and again, for long stays, always.

That much was settled. Still it did not seem to solve her problem. And it did not, because Phil Cameron had become her problem. At this stage of pondering she always threw up her hands. To give him up was unthinkable, even if she wanted to, which was indeed very far from her desires. That part did not perplex Kay. She thought she was waiting for this Reno situation to end, when she was actually waiting for herself. What was the true state of her heart? As she dreaded to search it, as she put off and off the inevitable, she drifted farther and farther with Phil, the sweetness of their companionship when alone equalling the audacity and thrill of their appalling role before the Reno crowd.

In mid-May the desert was abloom with spring flowers, the fragrance and color of which enraptured Kay. She had been quick to grasp that the desert intensified everything. No where else had seen the vividness that burned in desert flowers, in desert colors.

This particular morning Phil sat in the

car, with a sheaf of unanswered reports and letters from his California ranch on his lap, and instead of attending to them he watched Kay. She was aware of it. When she was far enough away not to see the yearning, the tragedy in his eyes, the havoc in his lean pale face (for his tan had long gone) she found pleasure in his watching her. But on occasions like this, when she came back to him, she always fell prey to a wild unconsidered impulse to tell him there might not really be any reason to dread the future. She had a secret that she had not yet divulged to herself. If she voiced it, made it tangible, then she would have to reckon with it, to try to explain it to an overwhelmed young man. And Kay was not ready for that.

Kay resisted a strong desire to steal away on the desert to a lonely spot far from the road, and there under the white sun, look out to the wasteland for an answer to her problem. The rocks, the sage, the flowers, the cacti, the flint ridges and the dry arroyes, the wide heat-veiled stretch leading to the encompassing mountains, spear-pointed and aloof against the sky — all these called her, almost availingly. How splendid and incomprehensible that such a solitude, such a lifeless area, could be pregnant with spirit. Kay felt it, and almost understood it, and feared it because it spoke to her of the uselessness and barrenness of her life. Should she flee from it as from a pestilence or embrace it with all her soul?

"Phil," she said, as she returned to him and the car with her hands full of desert wild flowers, "I've had some beautiful thoughts that no one at home would believe could dwell in Kay Hempstead's head, and that time-killing, divorce-waiting crowd back in Reno could not credit to Hilda Wales, mysterious adventuress and notorious woman."

"Yeah. I'm about fed up on that outfit, Kay," he replied, gloomily. "When I know you're as good as you're lovely. I damn near told Mom the whole story the other night when she called me a low-down bum that the toughest cowboys would scorn — and you a rich hussy."

"Phil, it hurts you, I know," returned

Kay, earnestly. "Because you're a man. But somehow it doesn't bother me in the least, I forget it the moment we get away together."

"But, how *can* you?" queried Phil, desperately.

"I know that it's not true, not one word of all the rotten gossip we have created. I know that our debauchery, as mother called it, does not exist. I know that the game has been in a good cause, which we've almost won."

"Ahuh. — Well, I've had a couple of thoughts, too. Not very beautiful. If you don't care a damn whether or not this shame follows you, then you've got it beat. What people think cain't hurt you if you don't let it. And that's that. . . . But how about me?"

"Phil!" she flashed, turning to him.

"Yes, Phil! . . . . You know I wouldn't give a whoop for gossip. I could go to my ranch, or back to the Arizona range and never heah a word of it again. What misery I've had has been solely that *you* have been dishonored in the eyes of this cheap Reno crowd."

"Then why ask 'how about me'?"

"Kay in some way you're not understandable. You're ice and flint. But God, you've been wonderful to me. Only I've been thinking what's to become of me? Could *any* man, much less a western fellow like me who never had serious love affairs, live with the loveliest girl in the world, be seen everywhere with her by hungry-eyed jealous hombres, dance and eat and gamble and play with her, and come out to the quiet desert with her, where she's her true self — could any man do that and get over it? . . . . You've kissed me, Lord knows seldom enough, but you *have* — and you've lain in my arms like that night in the moonlight, and most terrible of all, you haven't had any conscience or modesty, or anything, about how you let me see you, all but undressed; you've stayed under the same roof with me day and night — After this — this is over, which'll be soon now, do you think I can *live* without all that?"

Kay put a hand on his strong brown one, as it clenched the wheel, and she looked straight ahead out across the desert, which would have answered this very question for her, if she had had the courage to ask.

"Phil, it didn't seem so terrible — the aftermath — when we undertook this thing," replied Kay, gravely. "I was so obsessed I wouldn't face the cost. But now I begin to see the wrong I've done you."

"No. No," he interrupted. "I cain't see any wrong to me. I'm no child. My eyes were wide open. But it'll seem like being thrust out of heaven. . . . Aw, Kay, don't cry. I'll take my medicine."

"But I am the one that should have to take it," replied Katherine, as she wiped the tears from her eyes. "And despite everything we must not weaken on the main issue."

When they returned to town there was a message for Katherine. Victor Brelsford had arrived from New York and desired an interview with her.

"Brelsford is here, Phil," explained Kay, and handed him the message. "Mother sent for him. It's a complication that will be a boomerang for her."

"Yeah. Mr. Victor Brelsford, the swell

hombre who's going to marry you," returned Phil, in his cool drawl. But his eyes were on fire with Jealousy.

"He is not. I told you, Phil. I'll tell him instantly, if he broaches that old subject. Does that satisfy you?"

"Aw, I believe you — trust you, Kay," he rejoined. "I'll bet my soul you're on the level. . . . But I *cain't* be satisfied."

"You've been happy, for the most part. What would satisfy you?"

"Kay, I've concealed it from you," he said, hoarsely. "But since that night in the moonlight I've — I've been mad for your kisses."

"Is that all? Why didn't you take them, then?" she retorted, with a bewildering smile. "I confess to a hankering for yours."

Phil stared with starting eyes; his face turned red, and then went pale.

"We'll have a long while to — to enjoy each other's kisses. Let's forget that, too, for the present. Brelsford's coming will upset mother terribly. Because I'll refuse him finally, irrevocably. She has wanted me to marry into the Brelsford family more than she ever wanted anything. . . . I'll change my clothes and meet him for luncheon. You call for me, say in an hour. Look and be your western self, darling. We can't fool Brelsford."

A little later Katherine met Brelsford in the lobby of the Reno. His faultless correctness and his fair blase face brought back New York vividly. That first reaction of Kay's was a comparison, not greatly favorable to her own class. After the greeting, she led him to the drawing room, to a secluded corner.

"Mother sent for you?"

"Yes. A frantic appeal for help, it seemed to me. I had my doubts, but of course I came."

"I'm glad, Victor. After all, you are a friend of the family. Mother precipitated the mess and I've made it worse. Have you seen her?"

"I was with her for two hours. An ordeal, by Jove! She's a wreck, Kay. She poured out a long dissertation on your primrose path to degradation. And the epitome of it was that I rescue you before you sank into the gutter."

"By the sacrifice of your good name and position, I presume," replied Kay, with sarcasm.

"Kay, I didn't believe all that trash. Besides, if it were true I'd still repeat the proposal I've made you so often."

"Thank you, Vic. You're loyal and fine. I wish I could accept it. But since I came west I am — well, on the trail of my real self. Once more, and definitely, Vic, with infinite regret and appreciation of the honor, I must say no."

Flushing, he bowed silently to that decree.

"You can still be my friend without betraying mother. I hope you will be."

"Always, Kay."

"That increases my regrets. But, Vic, tell me what do you make of this situation?"

"I'm puzzled and bewildered. Disgusted with your mother, of course, as everybody is. Amazed at you — and frankly, now I've seen you, up in the air."

"Have you seen Leroyd?"

"No. And don't desire to."

"What have you heard about me?"

"Oh, gossip, here and there," he replied, evasively. "There seems to be a conflict between Kay Hempstead and an actress, Hilda Wales. That you were masquerading under her name, going Hollywood, and a lot of rot. You may be sure it never affected any of your friends who know you."

"Vic, I have to confess some of that gossip has foundation. I'm going to trust you now and tell you the truth."

Whereupon Katherine related in detail her plot to frighten her mother into abandoning her desertion of the family; and also what relation Phil Cameron and his mother bore to the situation.

"By Jove! It'd take Kay Hempstead to invent such a scheme and to carry it out," declared Brelsford, both intrigued and astounded. "Very clever of you. Then, as I suspected, all this — this rotten talk about you — your flagrant immorality, you know, is just what you worked for, and has no true grounds?"

"Precisely, Victor. It is a colossal bluff, and is going to succeed."

"Kay, I don't blame you. I uphold you.

What do you want me to do?" he rejoined, warmly.

"Go to mother. Be utterly shocked and heartbroken over my depravity. Assure her that you would not marry me now if I threw myself at your feet. Convince her that *she* is to blame for my revulsion against mothers, husbands, homes, and that if she does not come to me and promise to give up these divorce proceedings, you are absolutely certain that I will be utterly lost, damned forever."

Brelsford laughed. "What a beautiful devil you are, Kay! I'll do it. I'll give her the damndest raking over on my own score. And then do your bidding to the top of my bent."

"Vic, what a good sport you are!" exclaimed Kay, radiantly. "I'll be everlastingly in your debt. . . . Come now, let's hie ourselves to luncheon. I'm famished."

"Kay, wait a minute. In the dynamic whirl of your presence, I forgot the young man. Phil Cameron. What of him? What kind of a fellow?"

The keen intuition of a jealous and vanquished lover became obvious to Kay.

"He's western. Comes from good old pioneer stock. He rode the range for years, before going to California with his father, where they have large holdings in vineyards and orchards. He's twenty-six years old, a stunning looking boy, the finest and cleanest I ever knew."

"Well! You are enthusiastic — and for once you eulogize a member of my sex. I'd like to meet Cameron. If he's all you claim, Kay, then you are playing him a rotten trick."

Hot blood leaped stingingly to Katherine's very temples. The truth, spoken and not without a hint of contempt, by a gentleman, and one of her class, found the mark.

"Rotten! . . . . Why so unpleasant word, Victor?"

"You can't tell me this boy is not in love with you," declared Brelsford. "I wouldn't believe you if you did. For I know what it means to be with you. And if you're living with Cameron — in a cottage — alone. . . . *Whew!*"

"Please elucidate the whew, Victor," demanded Kay, coldly, with a level glance at him. "I made you my confidant. I didn't lie about Phil or our intimacy."

"Forgive me," he returned, hastily. "I didn't insinuate that you lied. The blood just went to my head. That explains the *'whew.'* . . . . But see here, Kay Hempstead, you should be told things. You have the old Helen beauty that is enough in itself. To see you is to worship. But to see you in all your outrageous shameless lack of modesty — that would be too much for any man. You simply should be torn to pieces."

The language of compliment was always wine to Kay's senses.

"Why, Victor, do you imagine I disrobed before Phil as Aphrodite did before Paris?" she asked, gayly.

"If you felt like it — and the flowers in the grass enhanced the color of your skin — you would."

"Oh, Victor. I don't think I'd ever go to such lengths to satisfy my vanity. . . . Still, I confess my immodest failing and will be careful to inhibit it in the future."

They went in to luncheon, where, when they had nearly finished, Phil found them. The introduction must have been trying to both men, but to Kay's surprise and pleasure the Westerner had a cool courteous poise that became him mightily. He was on his mettle, aware that in Brelsford he confronted all of Kay's alien and antagonistic world. Contrary to what might have been expected, Cameron's simplicity and the elder man's perspicuity and thoroughbred genuineness quickly brought the two into sympathy.

Kay grasped the opportune moment, and pleading a little shopping to do, she left them together. But from the store she went directly to her cottage, and changing to pajamas she lay down on her bed to rest and think. The gambling dens would save money that afternoon, she reflected, with a smile. There was much to ponder upon, but Kay did not get very far with it, before she fell asleep.

Phil awakened her, coming in at five o'clock. He appeared excited and enthusiastic, and sat down beside her on the bed, something he had not done before.

"Say, Kay, this old flame of yours is some swell guy," declared Phil. "He's shore a regular fellow. I like him to beat the band. We've been all over town, playing faro, monte, roulette. I won a lot. It shore tickles me when I beat these Reno games."

Kay sat up to give him a little pull toward her and a searching look.

"You've been drinking champagne, Phil," she said, severely. "I forbade that, you know."

"But, honey, only one bottle, and Brelsford ordered it."

"You should have confined yourself to one glass. We're to dine with Victor tonight and that means more champagne."

"Aw, don't worry about me. I can hold my liquor. . . . Dog-gone-it, Kay, I feel great. Somehow, without saying so outright, your friend made me feel the bigness of my responsibility for you — the — the privilege I had — and that, since you had to pull such an awful stunt, I was the man to trust."

"You are, Phil. And Brelsford saw it and was man enough to convey it without flattering you. Oh, I'm glad he came — glad you like him. . . . Right now he'll be giving mother the unhappiest hour of her life."

"I'll say he will. I was there when they met, in the lobby, just now. Would you believe it, Brelsford had the nerve to introduce me to her? 'Kay's cowboy friend,' he said. And if looks could slay, I'd be daid now."

"Vic said that? Oh, delicious! — Funny how life works out. Mother always hated cowboys because I loved to read about them — preferred western heroes to dukes and fairy princes."

"Sounds like poetic justice to me — Kay Hempstead falling for a cowpuncher who's far from a hero."

"Oh! So she's fallen for you, has she?" rejoined Kay, demurely. The boy was out of his head. "Don't tell it outside the family or it'll be front page news for our campaign."

"Kay, I gotta tell you the rest," he burst out, joyously. "I met Mom, too, and she's licked. Aw, but I wanted to hug her. She said she'd go back to Dad and forgive him — forget it all — if I'd only give up that beautiful half-naked glory-eyed vampire I was traveling around with!"

"Oh, Phil! — *No?*"

"Yes, by thunder! If it didn't hurt so, I could laugh till I cried."

"She called me all that? — Phil, I just loved her, too. But she's justified. . . . And what did *you* say?"

"I said I couldn't go back on you now — that you loved me — that I alone could keep you from the streets and dancehalls. Oh, a lot of bunk like that. She wept. She said: 'I'll send for your Dad. He'll fix this bad woman!' . . . . Aw, it's just too rich. If Dad comes and gets one look at you — the fire will be out."

"Phil, mother, too, is collapsing. When Vic gets through with her then the fire will be out there, too. . . . Oh, Phil, to the victor belong the spoils!"

"I don't get you, Lady," replied Phil, dubiously. "Brelsford's name is Victor."

"Your head isn't clear, darling. You'd better sleep or rest a while. . . . If you are very decorous and gentle about it, you may collect one — or more — of those kisses you raved about.''

That night at dinner Phil was not proof against the portent of the hour, the glamour of Kay's starlike eyes and lovely person, of later assurance of his mother's poignant capitulation. He drank far too much champagne. He hugged Kay so shamelessly that she forgot her role, for once, and refused to dance again with him. It amused Brelsford. Yet gave him a pang. For Kay divined that he thought there would be a tragic end to this farce. ''Get that boy home,'' he advised while they were having their last dance. ''He's true blue — too fine a lad for your sophisticated and decadent little comedy — drama. Cut the rest of your notoriety stunt. You can't undo the wrong you've done Cameron. But square it somehow. . . . I'll go up to your mother. I predict unqualified retrenchment for her.''

On the way out Phil bore himself well and appeared to be none the worse for his excess drinking. But the cold desert air, after the warm langorous atmosphere of the hotel, affected him so powerfully that he was drunk before they got back to their cottage. It was well that Kay had taken the wheel.

Phil stumbled indoors at her heels, breathing heavily, flushed of face. In the living room, where Kay let fall her furs, Phil made at her with a boyish ardor that yet had more heat and violence in it than he had ever exhibited. Kay let him take her in his arms, grief knocking at her heart.

"Phil, dear, you're drunk."

"Whosh drunk? . . . . Sweetie, I'm jus' gonna muss you all up."

"Not this gown, Phil. It won't stand pawing. . . . Kiss me and go to your room."

"Shore, I'll kiss you — all right — but I ain't gonna go. . . . Swell dress, Kay, but you jus's well might have nothun on. . . . B' gosh, I'll take it off. . . . Wash you pushin' me for? . . . . Say, Lady, I'll show you how I used to break — wild filly."

There was good-natured humor about him that seemed to be succumbing to something raw and elemental. But he lost coordination between mind and muscle. He lost his violence and his hands dragged at her, while he panted heavily, and sleepily closed his eyes. Then he slumped down on the couch, nearly carrying Kay with him. To her intense relief his collapse obviated any further concern for herself, although in spite of his being drunk, she did not believe she had anything to fear from him. She blamed herself for his condition. While she removed his coat, and collar and tie, and then his shoes, her mind worked swiftly. She recalled what Brelsford had advised. She must begin to undo the mischief, if that were humanly possible. How terrible it would have been for his mother to have seen him there! Then she put a pillow under his head. When he awakened, she thought, he would have some faint recollection of his condition. She would use that, exaggerate it, in order to make it a lesson. Then an inspiration seized her that, outrageous as it seemed, irresistibly took hold of her.

Dead asleep as he was, she had no trouble in stripping him to his underclothes. Then she scattered her furs, her purse and handkerchief, her slippers, on the floor before the couch, quietly overturned the table with its several objects, disarranged the rug, and otherwise made that side of the room suggestive of a considerable struggle. That done, she stared at her work, at her insensible victim, conscious of an inward burning vibration. Then without turning out the light, she went into her bedroom and locked the door.

Chapter 6

At intervals during the night Kay awoke, and late in the morning her last restless nap was disrupted by heavy sounds in the kitchen.

Phil was knocking about out there. His footfalls had not their usual light quickness. She heard the splashing of water and blowing expulsions of breath. Presently Phil growled to himself and then went out, his steps crunching the gravel path.

Sunlight, bright and golden, streamed in Kay's window, throwing shadows of moving leaves upon her bed. A mockingbird, the second Kay had ever heard, sang from the hedge. Kay's oppression and the misgivings of the black night vanished like mist before the sun. A presentiment of what she knew not, vague and boding, did not hold in her consciousness.

Kay reached for her make-up box and mirror, which she had placed near at hand. Then propped up by pillows, she began a careful and elaborate preparation that must preserve her beauty and at the same time give her face and eyes the counterfeit of terrible havoc. "Not such a task at that," she mused, ruefully. "I show my troubles." She pulled the blind down a little, to shade the sunlight somewhat, and composed herself to wait for Phil. And now that the hour was at hand — what would she say to Phil? Dare she go through with such a monstrous deceit? The injustice, the devilishness of her plan, the creed of noblesse oblige — all these shook her but did not change her. A stronger instinct, not wholly clear at the moment, held her tinglingly to her purpose.

Presently Phil's step, quick now, grated on the walk, and Kay sat up with her heart pounding in her breast.

He entered through the kitchen and came into the living room, where he halted with a sudden hard breath, like a gasp. What construction had he put upon the disarray of Kay's belongings, of the disorder of the room? Kay's courage almost failed her. But it was too late now. When Phil stamped to her bedroom door and knocked she did not have the voice to answer. He tried the door, to find it locked. He knocked louder and called fearfully: *"Kay!"*

"Oh! — Who's — there?" she replied, weakly.

"Who'n hell would it be?" he said, impatiently. "Open this door."

"What for?"

"I want to see you."

"You think you do — but you don't, Phil Cameron."

This occasioned a long silence, during which, no doubt, poor Phil's fears were confounding him.

"Kay! . . . damn it! — I must see you."

"Promise not — to — to touch me."

"Yes, I promise," he replied, harshly.

Kay slid out of bed, and unlocking the door, quickly ran back again.

Phil did not move for a moment. Then with violence he turned the knob and swept the door wide. As if the threshold had been an insurmountable wall he halted there, stricken by his first sight of her.

"Aw — Kay!" he cried, huskily, as if imagined fears had become realities.

Kay gazed back at him, with all that was true in her feeling for him, mingled with all the reproach and anguish she could muster.

"I — I was drunk — last night," he went on, brokenly.

She nodded her head in slow and sad affirmation.

"Did I — mistreat you?"

She turned her face away from his entreating look. "Phil, it was all my fault."

"My — God!" he gasped, and stumbled across the threshold to fall on his knees beside her bed, his head bowed, his hands clenching the coverlet. "I remember — something. . . . I wanted to undress you — meant to. . . . But I didn't think anything — lowdown. . . . It was that champagne . . . made a beast of me. . . . I didn't know — what I was about. . . . Aw!''

And he writhed in his shame.

"Phil, I am to blame," she said, softly, checking her arms from folding around his neck.

"Shore you are. But that doesn't excuse me," he said, and without any move to touch her, he slowly arose to his feet and stood staring down at her. "I'm sorry, Kay. That'll be about all for us. I cain't be trusted. I'm a — a — low-down dog! There's nothing for me to do but get out of here pronto."

"Phil! . . . . Hush! You mustn't talk that way," she cried, swiftly realizing her mistake. He was a grim man now, despising himself, and capable of any rash deed. It was the West in him, the desert breed of him, that lacked materialism and loathed sensuality. In one instant more Kay realized how unselfishly and purely she was loved. It seemed to exalt her — to lift her above her morbid phantasma, her inexplicable exactions.

"This game we played was crazy," he declared, his eyes like pale flames. "You should have known better — unless you — aw! hell, I cain't think that. . . . But I wasn't man enough to resist you. I gave in. We played the game. . . . Look at you! — and heah I am, sickened to death. All for what?"

"For our mothers, Phil."

"Aw, to hell with your mother! She wasn't worth it, nor mine either — the bull-haided old woman!"

"Come here, *Phil!*" cried Kay, imperiously, and she held out her arms.

At that juncture there came a solid knock on the living room door, which was at the front of the cottage. The disruption brought Phil and Kay back to time and place, and the uncertainties of their position. Kay stared up at him, while Phil slowly turned toward the door. A second knock followed, heavier than the first, carrying an aggressive note.

Phil crossed the room: "Who's out there?" he called.

"Hello. Is this where Kay Hempstead

stays?'' called a resonant masculine voice.

Kay heard it, recognized it, and sprang up with a startled cry.

"Yes," replied Cameron.

"Is she in?"

"Yes. But not to reporters."

"Mister cowboy, I'm no reporter," came the militant retort. "You'll find that out quick."

"Hell you say," muttered Phil, his cold visage reddening, and he checked a sudden move to open the door. "Who are you? What do you want?"

"Tell Kay that Jack Morse from New York is here to see her."

Phil did not need to inform Kay what she had heard as well as he. She arose, donned a dressing gown and hastened to the front door.

"Is it really you, Jack Morse?" she asked, in surprise.

"Kay! — yes, it's Jack in the flesh. You'll see when you open this door."

"But Jack — please excuse me. . . . I'll meet you at the Reno in half an hour."

"You'll see me right now, Kay Hempstead, if I have to smash

open this door."

At that Kay's color receded to leave her white, and she stood undecided, her brow puckered, and with anger apparently overcoming her amazement. Phil laid a powerful hand on the doorknob.

"Well, I'll see who the hell this hombre is," he declared, and he flung open the door.

Kay had Morse vividly in mind before he brushed into the room, so that his virile presence, his great bulk and dark visage added little. But his sombre and questioning mien gave her a shock. Morse, in his champion athlete days, not long ago, had been Kay's hero, so far as football went. She had coquetted with him then had kept up the friendship afterward. He, like Brelsford, was a friend of her family, and he had pressed his suit with all the rush and vim for which he had been famous in his University. But he had no claim whatever on Kay, and she resented this intrusion, the source of which she divined was her mother's frantic call for help.

Morse's contemptuous glance flashed

over Phil to alight upon Kay, and there it changed markedly. Phil quietly shut the door behind him, and stood back, his eyes narrowed to piercing slits.

"Jack, now that you have forced yourself in here, kindly explain your uncalled for action," said Katherine, coldly, omitting any greeting.

"Your mother wired me. I came by plane," replied Morse.

"That could be your only excuse, of course. But you should have sent me a message and arranged to meet me at mother's hotel."

"I just came from her. I couldn't wait. It was impossible to believe her. I had to see for myself."

"What?"

"If it is true that you are living openly with a cowboy."

"Quite true," returned Kay, without a flicker of an eyelash.

"Are you — married?" went on Morse, hoarsely.

"That is none of your business. But I'll tell you. No."

"It's true then, what she told me?

You've disgraced her — brought the name of Hempstead to disrepute — become a gambler, an adventuress, lost to common decency, the companion of a cheap cowboy?''

Phil sprang forward, furious at Morse's insulting words, but Kay laid a restraining hand on his arm. ''Wait, Phil,'' she commanded in no uncertain tone. Then turning again to Morse, she said, ''All true, Jack, except the cheap applied to my lover.''

Those cool words, almost flippant, acted like a lash upon Morse.

''You do not introduce me?'' he queried, insolently.

''No. That isn't necessary or desirable, since you insult me.''

''Insult *you?* For the love of —. The more I see of women the less I understand — and respect them!''

''I am not interested in your opinions. And I must request of you, now that I have frankly clarified any doubts in your mind as to my status, to please take yourself back to my mother. Tell her that I said the honor of the Hempsteads was her concern before it was mine, and as she chose to disregard it, I don't see why I shouldn't do as I please. She knows what kind of a man Leroyd is, and that she's making a fool of herself over him. He's after her money. He's gambling some of it away here in Reno."

"Well. . . . Who is decent these days? I shall dispense with any further interview."

"Jack, a graceful final gesture on your part would be to pan mother unmercifully."

"Okay. If I have any stuff left after I get through with you — and this western pup. . . . Final gesture you say? Well, it won't be graceful."

"Don't try to bully me, Mr. Morse. You always tried it and you never succeeded. Nor do I care to hear any of your bombast, for which you are famous."

"Kay, you're going to hear some of it straight," he said, angrily.

"Oh, am I? Well, first let *me* tell you your motive. You're a jealous man, and you want to vent your jealousy on me, before Cameron, because I preferred him as a lover to you as a husband."

Kay's taunt found an immediate main, showing that she had gauged with unerring and merciless precision.

"He's welcome to you, by God!" rasped the Easterner, stridently. *"You, who were once Kay Hempstead, now a strumpet. Why you look like a — like a street-walker —"*

Cameron leaped forward and whirled Morse so savagely that he staggered.

"Turn round, you!" he shouted, and his tawny hair stood up like the mane of a lion. "Western men don't talk that way to women. Out heah we'd call you a low-down city skunk!"

Then Phil lunged out, to strike Morse a terrific blow on his sneering mouth. The Easterner, staggering, took the table crashing down with him. His sudden fall shook the cottage.

Kay did not cry out, though she ran to the door of her bedroom, meaning to shut herself in. But she did not. Morse bounded up nimbly for so big a man. Blood gushed from his split lip, over his chin, and down on his white collar. Passion had dominated him, but the smash in the face eased and cooled him off. His training had been to fight. Physical violence was a stimulant, not a deterrent.

"Cowboy, I'll beat you half to death for that," he ground out, and made at Phil.

Kay could not take her fascinated gaze from the ensuing fight. At first as the contestants began to swing and slug, she welcomed the rawness of these two animals fighting over her. The age-old combat! It liberated something hot and vicious in her, feelings she had never experienced. She was a barbarian and gloried in this lithe, powerful stripling in unequal conflict with a giant. Phil was the nimbler on his feet. He landed oftener with his fists. But his blows did not tell upon his adversary as had the first one. He beat Morse about the face, but could not floor him again. On the contrary, Morse knocked Phil down repeatedly. The former began to whistle for his breath while the latter panted. Both began to sweat, which added to the flow of blood. They fought all over the living room, demolishing the furniture.

Kay's fierce sensory perceptions yielded to the intelligence of a woman who had seen many contests of strength and endurance, some of which had been real prizefights. She grasped that the combatants were unequally matched. Phil was being terribly beaten. Yet he fought back with all his might and main.

"Oh, Jack!" she cried, frantically, "that's enough. It's not fair. You're twice his size. . . . You'll kill him!"

But Morse, deaf to her entreaty, if he heard it, rushed Phil, beat him back with right and left, then swung a sodden blow that propelled him into a corner. Phil rolled over with a sucking intake of breath and rose, leaning on one hand. Between the hard breathing of the fighters, Kay heard the blood dripping from Phil's lowered face.

"Cowboy — you can — take — it — I'll tell the world," panted Morse, and he kicked his fallen rival. "But, by God! — you're whipped too bad — to lie in your sweetie's arms — again very soon."

"I'm whipped plenty — your way,"

replied Phil, thickly. "But wait a minute."

Morse righted a chair to sag into it. He mopped his lip which still bled. Kay stood in the door of her bedroom, staring at the prostrate Phil. She felt bursting to cry out, to run to him, yet she remained immovable and mute. She divined that this fight was not ended.

Phil got up, quickly it appeared, for one so battered, and staggered into the kitchen. Before Kay could unclamp her faculties Phil came back with a gun in each hand. He confronted Morse to toss the left hand gun into his lap.

"There, you slugger," he said, his voice like ice. "We'll take a fly at it western fashion."

"What — at?" bellowed Morse, fumbling with the big blue gun. Except for bruises and blood-stains his face went deadly white. "You mean — shoot it out?"

"That's what I mean, Mr. Morse."

"But Cameron — you — I. . . . There's no call — for murder."

"No, if you've got any guts. But if you haven't there'll be murder. . . . For I'm going to kill you — you big loud-mouthed bruiser — you filthy-minded Easterner! The West hasn't changed. You cain't get away with your vile insults — to her. Not out heah, Mr. Morse. . . . Throw that gun — you — before I bore you!"

It was then that Kay burst out of her paralyzed inaction, to find her senses and her spirit. She ran to Phil — almost brushing her breast with his leveled gun.

"Phil! — For God's sake — wait — listen!" she implored.

"Get out of my way, Kay. I don't want to kill you, too."

"Darling, you can't kill him. It'd be murder. *He* won't fight with a gun. He's afraid for his life."

"So it looks. But no matter. I don't care a damn." Bloody and magnificent he stood, not the boy Phil she had known but a ruthless man in whom the heritage of the West called its fierce law. She sensed more than his succumbing to the creed of cowboy and pioneer. He welcomed this fight and the chance to force Morse to shoot him as a means to the end he believed he deserved.

"Listen to me or I'll fight you for this gun," flashed Kay, as she seized it with both hands.

"Let go. That's a hair trigger. It might go off."

"Will you listen?" she besought him, faintly.

"Yes, if you'll let go my gun."

She released her hold on it and swayed against his breast, which support she needed until she could rally. The unexpected contact of her disengaged his attention from Morse. Kay felt him shake. That moment was one of revelation. A strong and welling current of blood raced back from her heart to revive her. With her arms sliding up around him, her hands locking behind his neck, all doubt, all uncertainty ceased for her, and she knew that this moment of her surrender to her love would save him and herself.

"Phil, we have made mistakes," she began, eloquently, "but do not crown them by a tragic deed, that would result in death for you and terrible misery for me. You are furious now. Not because Morse whipped you. What is that to you? He's twice your size and a slugger besides. Nor should you want to kill him because of what he called me. He thinks it's true. But *you* know it's false. . . . Moreover, you are laboring under a delusion about what happened last night. It — didn't happen! — I just helped you to believe so for a silly reason of my own. All this has faced me with the real truth. I love you, Phil. I am yours. I could not go back east without you, if I ever go. . . . For the rest, what does that matter? My mother's trouble — your mother's — for which we disgraced ourselves to shame them, these matter little beside our own problem, which, darling, will be a problem no longer the moment you see the truth."

Kay felt Phil's arm over her shoulder, as evidently he made a move with the gun toward Morse.

"Get out and don't butt into me again," he ordered, curtly.

Kay heard Morse thump the gun on the floor, then his dragging footfalls. He opened the door, shuffled out and closed it.

"Kay, I hope he gets out of town before

117

I recover from the talk you gave me. It was shore some talk. . . . My God, what a woman can be and do! . . . . But that saved his life. I reckon mine, too."

She lay against him, exhausted. And whatever his doubt, his uncertainty, he found her warmth and sweetness and surrender beyond his power to withstand.

"Phil, it was true — all I said," she replied, presently, in an unsteady voice.

"Aw! — You've won, Kay. Don't rub it in. . . . Lately I've reckoned you cared for me. But I couldn't believe it. You must now."

"Care for you? My dear boy, I love you — love you as I never loved anyone in my life."

"After last — night?" he whispered in her hair.

"Especially after last night."

"Oh, Lord! — But I cain't be happy — I cain't ever."

"Phil, didn't I tell you that you were wrong about what you think happened when you were drunk?"

"Yes, I heahed you. It's a beautiful lie, my dearest. You're as noble and forgiving as you are lovely."

"I didn't lie. I swear to God."

"Kay! Don't perjure your soul."

"Oh, you obstinate cowheaded cowboy!" cried Kay, beside herself. "If you love me, why won't you believe me?"

"I'm beginning to grasp the greatness of a woman."

"You drive me desperate. I'll give you one more chance. Do you — will you believe me?"

"No, sweetheart, I cain't."

"Very well then," she retorted, and deliberately she raised her lips close to his with a low laugh.

"Don't play with me, Kay."

"I'm in dead earnest. . . . Must I coax for kisses?"

"Kay! — with this bloody nose?" he expostulated, half frantic.

"Darling, I didn't ask you to kiss me with your nose," she said, and taking his handkerchief from his hand she tenderly wiped the bleeding member.

"I must be a sight. My lip's cut. My face hurts all over."

She kissed his twitching mouth, which

was suspiciously carmine in hue, and then the several bruises on his face. "There! That ought to soothe the pain. . . . You don't look so very bad. . . . Phil, I think by the dexterous use of my make-up, I can make you presentable — for our honeymoon."

"Mercy!" he gasped.

Then seriously she told him every little detail that had happened the night before upon their return to the cottage, and as for her motive, she bared her soul to explain that strange and eternal feminine urge.

"Darling, you give me back something — 'most as much as the promise of your dear self," he returned, solemnly.

"Come, let me wash the blood off you — and myself too! . . . . Oh, that big bully — how I hate him! Yet I ought to love him! He made me realize how I really love you!"

Chapter 7

On the eve of victory Kay and Phil forgot all about their mothers, forgot everything but the transport of their love, everything save their plan to be married and spend the honeymoon in Arizona before going on to California. To them divorce was a nightmare that had vanished in the sunlight of day. Marriage was the most beautiful dawning of a dream and glory, the consummation of all things, the hope and fulfillment of youth and life.

On the following day they were married by the famous minister of Reno, who joined together so many who, having failed once or twice, or even more, still followed the gleam.

"Phil, let us go inform our dear parents that as far as humanly possible we have made amends for our misconduct," said Kay, radiantly. "And that we shall spend the rest of our lives proving the absurdity of such a place as this Reno divorce-mill, and the joy and good of marriage."

They drove to the dealer from whom Kay had rented the car. She purchased it outright. Then they went to their cottage, and while Phil loaded their baggage in the back seat, Kay lingered in the rooms that had unconsciously grown dear. How seldom things affected her like this!

Phil dropped Kay at the Hotel Reno. "I'll take the car to the garage, pay some bills and be back pronto," he said. "I hope our glad news will finish your mother. It shore will Mom."

Kay went directly to her mother's apartment, striving for an indifferent mien, but eager to reveal the plot that had failed, and to confess her marriage. She found Mrs. Hempstead fully dressed and wholly devoid of some characteristic which Kay could not at once analyze.

"Oh, it's you, Kay. I thought you'd

come flaunting in pretty soon."

"Good morning, mother. I hope you are well," rejoined Kay, brightly.

"I'm as well as could be expected under the circumstances. I needn't ask after *your* health. You're a picture of it. And your old beautiful self! God in heaven, how can you burn the candle at both ends, yet still retain your infernal youth and beauty?"

"Mother, my recipe is simple," replied Kay, naively. "I eat and sleep properly, drink little wine and never cocktails, and keep my conscience clear."

"You have the impudence of your generation, my dear. . . . Get it over with."

"What?"

"You evidently came to crow over me in my degradation."

"Not at all. I came to make up with you, if you will — and to say goodbye."

"Leaving, eh? I thought Morse would jar you out of your love-nest, if Brelsford couldn't."

"Have you seen Jack since yesterday?"

"Yes, for a moment. He looked as if he'd been in an auto smash-up. And he acted queer, too. Said I was all wrong about you. Then he called me a decadent silly old dame, along with some more insulting things and left to catch his plane.''

"Morse hits hard, mother, as Phil and I well know. . . . Yes, you *are* all wrong about me. Listen to this." And Kay told her story, not sparing herself.

"Katherine Hempstead! You played that hoax on me — to save me? You disgraced yourself abominably to save me? All the time your atrocious conduct — your brazen immorality — was a sham — a trick to frighten me out of my rights?''

"All the time, mother, darling. I'm sorry, and ashamed now. But when I got here, I couldn't move you.''

"What's to become of the young man, Cameron? — Brelsford got acquainted with him, said he was a fine fellow, a gentleman, evidently of good family. That you had been as consciousless with him — wrecked his life, as you have so many men.''

"Consciousless, I confess. But I'm sure I haven't wrecked Phil. For this morning

124

I married him."

Mrs. Hempstead uttered a faint shriek and fell back from her upright dignity, into limp and abject prostration.

"You astounding — terrible young woman!" she ejaculated.

"Well, I'm settled, finally. I'm finished, mother — except for love, home, husband, babies, happiness. You ought to be glad. Father will be, and Polly."

"Thank God! This saves me. I want to know the cowboy who could work such magic in Kay Hempstead."

"You'll like Phil. He's not a cowboy any more. That range life was his youth. He's a California planter now."

"Does he know you're worth millions?"

"I'm sure not. Of course, he saw that I had money. I spent it right and left. Funny thing, mother, I couldn't lose. Whenever I gambled I won. I'm away ahead of the game. Fact is, I bought my car with Reno winnings."

"Well, I lost," declared Mrs. Hempstead, bitterly. "It was a lesson I needed. But you know, of course."

"I know nothing. What do you

mean by lost?"

"The money I brought with me. Some thousands. My jewels — all gone."

"Mother! . . . . Did Leroyd. . . ."

"You might not know he — appropriated my property. But you surely know he ran up a gambling debt of ten thousand dollars at Fillmore's private game."

"I don't surely know."

"But you must have seen this?" Mrs. Hempstead reached for a large purse on the table, from which she extracted a letter. This, with shaking hand, and shamed averted eyes, she gave to Kay. The envelope contained some kind of a report on a single page. The printed heading denoted a detective agency. The details were in type. Kay's swift gaze ran over a full record of Leroyd's philandering and gambling while in Reno.

"Kay, you were right. I apologize," said her mother, sadly. "Leroyd left day before yesterday, without a word to me."

"Well of all things! I hardly guessed he was a gentleman crook. . . . Oh, mother, how cheaply you got rid of him! Just think."

"Yes, cheaply, from a material point of view. . . . Kay, didn't you put a detective to watch Leroyd?"

"No, I never thought of such a thing. Honestly. Victor might have done it. But he never told me."

"He might have been just that clever. Fetch up your Westerner so that I can see what addition you have made to the Hempstead family. I sincerely hope *all* your sacrifices — your heedless wild actions have not been in vain."

Soberly Kay left her mother and went downstairs to meet Phil. But for her marriage she would have regarded the whole circumstance as an ironical joke on herself. Still there was Phil's mother to think of. And hoping that Phil's sacrifice of reputation would yet turn her back home, Kay crossed the lobby toward the drawing room, to come face to face with Mrs. Cameron.

Mrs. Cameron hung on the arm of a tall, wide-shouldered, extremely handsome man about whom there appeared something familiar. He had a bronzed clean-shaven face, wonderful eyes like gray daggers, and clustering chestnut hair whitened over the temples.

"Heah she is, Frank," announced Mrs. Cameron, grimly.

"Air you Miss Hilda Wales?" queried this man, perfunctorily, with marveling gaze sweeping her down and up.

"No," replied Kay, swiftly recovering her equilibrium, and she stood in smiling expectancy, with all her natural poise.

"Then you must be Miss Katherine Hempstead?"

"No."

Phil's father wrenched his fascinated eyes from the gracious object of his interrogation, and turned to the little wife.

"Mom, you're off the trail," he said, troubled. *"This* girl shore cain't be that. . . ."

"She is, Frank. I know her," declared Mrs. Cameron, vehemently.

"But she doesn't look like one of those painted Hollywood actresses," protested the rancher.

"Oh, you men! She *is* an actress. That's her business. It was her angel face that led our son astray. She could fool God

Almighty himself."

When Cameron turned to look again at Kay, he was plainly lost. In his eyes Kay read that if all this were true about her, it did not matter and he did not blame Phil.

"Mr. Cameron, I have the honor to inform you that I am Phil's wife and your daughter-in-law," said Kay, sweetly.

The horror and consternation that gripped Mrs. Cameron evidently did not extend to the steel-eyed rancher. But he was sorely at a loss, between the devil and the deep sea.

"Mrs. Cameron, if you'll listen, I'll tell you why it's not so very bad for Phil," said Kay, appealingly.

Just then Phil came running up opportunely, his face so happy that the sundry bruises and cuts detracted little from its comeliness.

"Dad!" he whooped, and made at his father, who certainly met him half way. "Heah with Mom! Aw, you shore look good to my sore eyes."

"Howdy, son. How'd you get bunged up?" replied the rancher, coolly, as he let go of Phil.

"Had a little scrap, Dad. Gosh, I'm glad to see you and Mom together again — and heah with Kay. Has she introduced herself?"

"Wal, I'm not shore, but I reckon she's Hilda Wales, Kay Hempstead and Mrs. Phil Cameron, all together. Am I correct?"

"Right Dad — and am I happy," flashed Phil. "Mom, get that scared sick look off your face. Dad, it's all too wonderful to tell."

"So I savvy. But would you mind clearin' up all this bunk Mom has been feedin' me, since I got heah?"

"It's not bunk, but romance, Dad. . . . I met Kay the night I got heah to Reno. We fell in love right then. At least *I* did. She had come out to stop her mother from divorcing her father. I had come to keep Mom from divorcing you. Well, we couldn't do a damn thing with either of our mothers. So we planned to throw the wildest stunt we could think of. We played to the gallery — gambled, drank, drove, danced, lived together, just two young folk clean gone to hell. All to sicken and scare Mrs. Hempstead and Mom out of their haids. . . . But, Dad, it was all a bluff. We played a swell game. Kay's friends came out and spilled the beans for us. They made us think of ourselves — that we couldn't go on. Besides we had the game about won. So this mawning we were married.''

''Wal, I'll be dog-goned,'' exclaimed the rancher, with a hearty laugh. ''Shore is some story. But couldn't you young folks have had all the romance *and* love without the shady stuff?''

Phil looked blank and somewhat crestfallen, while Kay began to see the light. If what she divined were true, then how cruelly had their agonies been wasted!

''Mom, you sent for Dad?'' asked Phil, eagerly.

''Indeed, I did not,'' returned his mother. ''He came without being asked.''

''Wal, son, I reckon I'd knuckled anyway, sooner or later,'' interposed the rancher, in his cool slow drawl, and his keen eyes twinkled from Phil to Kay. ''But the fact is Marcheta eloped with that greaser, Lopez. Left me cold. And

131

seein' the error of my ways, I hot-footed it to Reno to square myself with your mother.''

"Marcheta? The black-eyed little hussy! And *I* was fond of her!'' ejaculated Phil. Then awakening to the irony of his and Kay's past ventures, he turned to her: "What have we been up against? I just found out Leroyd ran off.''

"Yes. Mother told me,'' returned Kay. "She let me read the record from the detective agency. I thought it was Brelsford. Phil, were you responsible for that?''

"Shore. I got wise to Leroyd and put the detectives on his trail. They were to mail reports to him and your mother at the end of a week. I forgot it — like I forget everything else.''

"Making your mother suffer all for nothing!'' interposed Mrs. Cameron.

"No. I'll never believe that,'' declared Phil, stoutly. "But Kay and I — look what *we* did — how *we* suffered — all for nothing!''

"Not all, Phil,'' rejoined Kay, softly. "We found love. And the West has won me — saved me, no doubt."

"Wall, all's wal that ends wal. I reckon there'll be a tightenin' of loose bridles, and a long ride down to sunset," added the rancher, his fine dark face alight.

F